Red
& *the*
Wolfe

A Lake Okoboji Fable

by Jean Tennant

Shapato Publishing
Everly, Iowa

Published by: Shapato Publishing
              PO Box 476
              Everly, IA 51338

ISBN: 978-0-9826992-3-2
Library of Congress Control Number: 2010906862

This is a work of fiction. Though the Okoboji area exists as part of the Iowa Great Lakes, in this book the lake, the town, and businesses have been recreated for the author's purposes.

First Printing May 2010

The **Iowa Great Lakes** is a group of natural glacial-carved lakes in Northwest Iowa. The three principal lakes of the group are Spirit Lake, West Okoboji Lake, and East Okoboji Lake. They're the largest natural lakes in the state of Iowa, with the largest, spring-fed Spirit Lake, being 134 feet deep. The area is often referred to simply as Lake Okoboji, and is one of Iowa's most popular vacation destinations in both summer and winter.

ONE

Riley Harrison sat in the booth, her hands framing the coffee cup, absorbing its warmth. She'd taken this seat so she could keep an eye on her car, out in the parking lot of the first coffee shop she'd spotted when getting off the interstate. But that also meant she had a clear view of all the snow and ice out there.

Driving on it had been bad enough.

Shivering, Riley turned away from the window. In the booth directly across from hers sat a man who'd wolfed down a meal that would've easily sustained her for days. Fascinated—and wondering where he put it—she'd sneaked the occasional glance in his direction.

The man pushed his empty plate away and leaned back, plaid shirt pulling taut across a broad chest and firm midsection. Then he looked over, and gave Riley a white-toothed smile that peeked out from the stubbly growth of a short brown beard.

Caught staring, Riley dropped her eyes to her cup, scolding herself for feeling flustered. But when he'd looked directly at her, she'd almost forgotten about the ice and snow outside.

Almost.

She sighed. No more putting it off. Her grandmother was expecting her. It was time to make the last leg of her trip. Picking up the new parka she'd bought especially for this week in Iowa, she headed for the cash register near the front door.

After handing her money to the woman at the register, Riley slipped her arms into the parka.

"You look familiar," the cashier said as she pulled change from the till. "Are you from around here?"

"No, just visiting," Riley told her.

The woman stared for a moment, then a broad smile played across her features. "Omigod! Riley Harrison—is it really you? It *is* you."

Eyebrows arching in surprise, Riley took her change. She hadn't been back to Iowa in several years. The woman had an open, friendly face with a scattering of freckles across an upturned nose, but there was nothing familiar about her. Or was there?

Something tugged at the back of Riley's mind, a memory that wanted to surface, but was hidden so far back in the shadows of her subconscious that it hadn't seen the light in many years. *Freckles . . . suntan lotion . . .*

She was still struggling with elusive recollection when the woman came out from behind the counter and, to Riley's utter astonishment, threw her arms around her. Caught off guard, Riley could only endure the embrace with open-mouthed astonishment, aware that the man from the booth had stepped up behind her and was watching them with a bemused expression.

When she was at last released, Riley almost stumbled backwards.

"How long has it been?" the woman asked enthusiastically, looking ready to lunge at Riley again.

Unable to hide her bewilderment, Riley could only mumble, "Um . . . I'm not sure."

The woman's cheeriness wavered. "You don't remember me, do you? It's *me*—Lauren Ross. Well, it was Lauren Winslow way back when we used to hang out together. That's been, what, twenty years? At least that, because I was twelve when my family moved here, and you were staying at your grandparents' summer resort."

"L-lauren?" Riley stammered. The old memory peeked out from the dim shadows. *Suntan lotion . . . giggling phone conversations . . . deep, meaningful discussions about the latest pop star . . .* "I do remember you. Wow. This is incredible."

"It sure is. I thought—wait a minute. Aaron, let me ring that up for you, we might be a minute here."

"I'm in no hurry." The man behind Riley spoke in a low

rumble of a voice, but he approached the counter and handed over his bill.

Still struggling to process this new information, Riley stepped to one side.

It'd been during the summer of her twelfth year that she'd come for her annual visit to her grandparents' lakeside resort, and had made friends with a skinny girl named Lauren. They'd spent a busy August splashing in the clear green water of the lake, trolling the sand for shells, whispering their innocent secrets and vowing to write to each other over the winter months. Their friendship had lasted through three summers, halted prematurely when Riley's visits to Lake Okoboji had ended. When she was fifteen Riley's parents had divorced. She'd stopped spending her summer months with her grandparents, and she'd all but forgotten Lauren, her friend in Iowa.

Now, here was Lauren. Older, as was Riley, but still freckle-faced and cheerful, her smile revealing the lively teenager she'd once been.

After paying his bill, the man at the counter gave Riley a friendly smile and moved aside, but seemed in no hurry to leave the coffee shop.

Turning again to Riley, Lauren pelted her with questions. "Do you still live in Texas?"

"Yes, but I'm in Dallas now."

"What do you do there?"

"I'm in web design."

"Cool. Married?"

"Nope. Never been."

Almost two decades fell away as they slipped easily into the verbal shorthand of those long-ago summers.

"I was, but not any more. I've been divorced for a couple of years now."

"I'm sorry to hear that," Riley said.

Lauren shrugged. "I'm better off without him, and I have two great kids. Are you here to visit your grandmother?"

Riley told her that she was. "I'll only be here for a week," she added. "But it's been a few years since I've been back, and I'm not sure I remember the way. What I *do* remember is how

9

easy it is to get lost on these roads."

"*That* hasn't changed. Here, I'll write down the directions for you."

But before Lauren could reach for a pen, the bearded man spoke up. "I'm headed in that direction. Follow me, Red—I'll take you right to it."

Riley winced. As a kid she'd endured the teasing that invariably befell redheads, but as she'd grown older her hair had deepened to a more acceptable auburn, and she'd hoped the nickname was behind her. Apparently not, and she almost ran her tongue over her teeth to see if the braces had returned as well.

Eying him, she said, "You know the way to my grandmother's house?"

"If you're talking about Bette Harrison, sure I do." His smile was slightly crooked, curving up more on one side than the other, his teeth straight and white. The stubble of beard and longish hair, combined with a flannel shirt beneath a casually opened jacket, gave him an untamed look that put Riley's city-girl guard up.

"All I need are directions," she insisted.

"This'll be easier." He was already opening the door, his crooked grin widening as though enjoying her discomfort.

Seeing her hesitation, Lauren spoke up. "It's okay, Riley. You can trust Aaron Wolfe. I'll vouch for him."

And so Riley's fate was sealed, though she wondered who would vouch for Lauren. She hadn't seen this woman since they were kids, yet here she was sending Riley off with a man who looked, as he towered in the open doorway letting all the cold air in, like someone Riley might otherwise have crossed the street to avoid. Seeing no way to gracefully refuse, Riley put her change in her pocket and stepped through the doorway.

"I'll call you later at your grandmother's house," Lauren called out. "We have lots of catching up to do while you're home."

Home. Riley almost turned around to correct her—this wasn't home, this was a visit—then thought, what the hell.

On the way to her car Riley's impractical shoes slid out

from under her. Arms pinwheeling, she yelped, "Whoa!" as she struggled to stay upright. She might have fallen, but Aaron Wolfe grabbed her around the waist, his arm as solid as an oak branch through her parka.

"Careful," he said, and held her tight.

"I'm okay," she gasped. She wanted to shake him off and tell him she could manage. She didn't need his help, didn't need anyone's help. She'd been doing things on her own for a long time. But his grip, for the moment, was the only thing keeping her upright. With no other choice than to cling to him, Riley looked up into his face, and when he grinned something inside her tumbled out of control.

Oh, my. What big teeth he had.

"You'll want to wear better shoes while you're here," he said. "Just for a week, is it?"

"That's right." Her words sounded shaky, which annoyed her, so she cleared her throat and added, more forcefully, "One week."

"That's too bad. That you're leaving so soon, I mean."

He continued to hold her close, and Riley had the distinct impression that he found her amusing. Sure, it was easy for him to laugh at the city girl who couldn't walk on ice. She wanted to push him away, but was afraid that if she did she would suffer the even greater indignity of landing on her butt.

He helped her the rest of the way to her car, then made sure she was safely inside before releasing her.

"Thanks," she muttered, reaching for her seatbelt.

"I'm parked right over there," he said. "Follow me. I promise to go nice and slow."

The way he looked at her made Riley's face flame. There had been something decidedly suggestive in that remark, but she only nodded and put her key in the ignition.

Determined to make the best of the situation, Riley dutifully followed him from the parking lot. His vehicle was a late model SUV, streaked with slush from the salted roads, an environmental gas-hog that was undoubtedly practical for winters in the Midwest.

When the SUV turned on a road that was not clearly marked and held no remnant of familiarity, she had to admit, if only to herself, that she wouldn't have chosen this route on her own. If Aaron Wolfe really did know his way around this heavily wooded area, it was probably a good thing she'd allowed him to lead the way. Not that she'd ever tell *him* that. She still sort of resented the way he'd moved right in on her conversation with Lauren.

But then she thought again about his strong arm, and the way he'd held her. Shaking her head, Riley forced away the feelings that brief contact had brought about. She was here to see her grandmother. This was not the time to be having unsettling thoughts about some guy who looked as though he hadn't shaved in a month.

After all, she was only going to be here for a week.

Aaron kept a watchful eye on the car in his rearview mirror as he drove the familiar roads around the west side of the lake. He kept his speed down to make it easy for her to keep up on the icy roads.

Running a hand across his chin, he wished now he'd shaved, but he was just getting back from a week-long stay at his cabin up north, where he tended to neglect such things. And of course he'd had no idea he'd be running into a pretty little redhead almost immediately upon his return.

"Riley." He said the name aloud, liking the way it sounded. It was an interesting name for a woman, and it suited her. She'd shown a flash of spirit when he'd let his arm creep a bit too familiarly around her waist, and he chuckled at the memory. Every muscle in her little body had tensed, coiling as tightly as a spring, and he'd been hard-pressed not to laugh out loud. He'd felt a tantalizing hint of womanly softness beneath her bulky clothing, which made him speculate as to what other hidden wonders might be waiting to be revealed.

This could be interesting. He'd been way too bogged down with business these past couple of years, with getting his restaurant up and running efficiently again after a near-bankruptcy. Since he'd taken it over, he'd been so wrapped up in work that he'd mostly neglected his social life.

Maybe it was time to relax and have some fun. Riley Harrison looked like she could be fun, and the best part was he didn't have to worry about a couple of casual dates turning into anything serious, which was the last thing he wanted.

After all, she was only going to be here for a week.

Aaaawoooo.

TWO

The road was slick in spots, and more than once the tires of Riley's car slipped. Only for a moment, but it was enough to make her heart flutter in her chest. Off to her right the ice-smooth surface of the lake peeked through the thick growth of trees. How strange, she thought, to see these trees without their summer foliage, like survivors of a once festive party, hung over and stripped of their fancy attire.

Even as a child she'd never visited her grandparents during the winter months, and Riley had to wonder now if it'd been wise to come. But she'd taken time off from work to travel through several states because, in their many telephone conversations, she'd detected an uncharacteristic frailty in her grandmother's voice that had raised a flag of alarm. If her concerns turned out to be groundless, well, that was great— she'd return home, satisfied that nothing was seriously wrong. If there *were* problems, she'd deal with them as best she could in the allotted time. It fell on her shoulders to make this trip because her sister Meghan had two small children to take care of, and their mother was currently on a singles cruise floating somewhere around the Bahamas, with the well-being of her former mother-in-law not a top priority. Riley and Meghan's father had died several years earlier.

As she drove, the trees grew less dense, and the houses along the lake's edge tugged at her memory. The area seemed to have grown and expanded, with upscale homes appearing along stretches of land that had been previously undeveloped.

These signs of new growth were deceptive, she knew. Her grandmother had kept her informed of the goings-on around Lake Okoboji. The real estate bubble had burst here a couple of years ago, as it had nearly everywhere else. Homes and businesses were in foreclosure. People had moved away to look for something better somewhere else, and few were moving in. In a resort town that depended heavily on summer revenue to carry its citizens through the winter months, a lagging economy could have disastrous results.

Rounding the last bend, Riley felt an ache of nostalgia. It wasn't that she hadn't seen her grandparents over the years. When her grandfather had still been living, he and Gran had made twice-yearly treks to Texas to see Riley and Meghan, their only grandchildren. And over the past several years Bette Harrison had made the trip many times on her own. But the last time Riley had been back to Lake Okoboji herself was more than six years ago, for her Grandpa Joe's funeral, and that had been in the early fall.

As the Harrison Lakeside Cottages came into view, Riley eased up on the gas pedal. The SUV was already parked in the driveway beside the house.

She pulled up beside it, her eyes drawn to the cabins, which seemed smaller than she remembered. The twelve small, one-bedroom units faced the lake. Each cabin was named after a bird indigenous to Iowa, with Golden Oriole and Purple Martin being the two closest to the beach. The trim of each was painted to reflect the colors of its namesake. Next to the cabins was her grandmother's house, the upstairs of which held a bedroom papered in pink roses, and a window that overlooked the lake.

But Riley wasn't looking at the house just yet. Her attention was on the cabins. The once-charming little units had an air of neglect about them that couldn't be entirely blamed on their winter emptiness. Shutters had worked loose and hung like crooked teeth, shingles were missing, and the paint was faded. Prairie Hen had a window in front that was cracked, a length of masking tape acting as a temporary patch that only drew attention to the flaw.

Aaron Wolfe got out of his SUV and walked toward her. She'd assumed he would continue on his way now that she was at her grandmother's house. Surely he had things to do, people to annoy. No such luck. His coat was still open despite the cold. He seemed oblivious to both the weather and her discomfort, his eyes appraising as they swept over her.

"While you're here you should stop at my restaurant, the West Woods," he said as he drew closer.

Riley looked at him. "You work in a restaurant?"

"I own a restaurant."

"Why were you eating at the coffee shop if you have your own place?" she couldn't resist asking.

"Because the Kozy Korner serves the best breakfast in town, and my place is strictly an evening business."

"Ah," she said. "Must be year-round then."

"That's right. Tonight would be a good night to come in. I can show you around."

"I don't know what my grandmother has planned," she told him. She tore her gaze away from his, breaking eye contact to regain control. Something about the way he looked at her made her feel naked, despite the multiple layers of clothing she wore.

"Bring Bette with you," he said. "She likes the food at my place."

There *was* something captivating about the man, she had to grant him that much. Now that she was more accustomed to the ruggedness of his appearance, he was even somewhat attractive. His eyes were his best feature, no doubt. Deep-set, hazel with flecks of gold, they turned up a little at the corners to give him a roguish appearance. Above those eyes were brows that drew together in a V that wasn't a frown so much as their natural shape. Broad shoulders gave him substance. A little over six feet, she guessed, and he seemed to fill the space around him—or suck the air out of it, she wasn't sure which, because as she looked into those penetrating eyes she felt her breath catch.

Before she could form a reply, the front door of the house opened and Bette Harrison stepped out onto the porch.

Riley hurried to the porch, ready to embrace the one person who'd always loved her unconditionally, but as she approached her grandmother, her step faltered. Though they talked on the phone at least once a week, it had been a while since Riley'd seen her. The strong, erect woman who'd always carried herself with an air of self-possession had aged. Her hair was grayer, too, and the effect added years to her appearance.

For the first time in Riley's memory, her grandmother looked her age.

She'd reached the front porch, still taking in this latest shock, when a bright smile broke across her grandmother's features.

"Oh, honey, you made it!" Bette Harrison held out her arms, and Riley rushed up the steps and into them.

Feeling again twelve years old as her grandmother's arms went around her, Riley inhaled the familiar scent of White Linen perfume.

"Let me see you." Bette held Riley at arm's length, and brushed a strand of hair away from her forehead. "I've always said you got your gorgeous hair from my side of the family." She put an arm around Riley's shoulders. "It's cold out here, let's go inside."

"I have a couple of bags..." Riley started to say. When she turned, however, she saw that Aaron Wolfe had opened the back seat of her car and taken out her two suitcases. He was already carrying them toward the porch.

"Bring those on in, Aaron," Bette said easily.

Carrying the suitcases past her on the porch, Aaron smiled genially at Riley, who was busy shooting eye-daggers at him. He bent his knees and groaned. "What d'ya have in here, bricks?"

Riley followed him inside. "Ha-ha. Very funny."

"You'll be staying upstairs in your old room," Bette told Riley.

Aaron made a move for the stairway. "I'll take these up for you."

"No need," Riley said.

Too late. He was already halfway up the stairs.

"I'll start some fresh coffee," Bette said, and headed for the kitchen.

When he reached the top of the stairs, Aaron looked into the first bedroom. Riley was still at the bottom, scowling up at him. "Is this the one?" he asked.

She sighed heavily and came up the steps. "You didn't have

to do that. I could have carried my bags upstairs myself."

"Of course you could have. But I wanted to help." He went into the bedroom and set the larger suitcase on the bed.

Riley followed him into the room. She stood with her arms crossed, looking everywhere but directly at him.

Aaron set the other bag down, and took a step toward her. He could see the shimmering highlights in her hair as the sunlight coming in through the window turned it to liquid fire. Her skin was pale and smooth, and he wanted to reach out and touch her cheek.

He moved very close to her, but kept his hands to himself. Alone with her here in this room, he didn't trust himself to make that physical contact he so wanted to initiate. If he started, he feared, he would fall into the deep well of those fathomless eyes, never to surface again.

"I should have listened to you," he murmured.

She did look up at him then, and it was almost his undoing.

"What?" Her voice was a whisper, as light as an evening breeze over the lake.

"I shouldn't have come up here." This wasn't a safe place for him to be. He had to get away. While he still could.

She seemed about to say something more, but Aaron quickly stepped around her and was out the bedroom door before she had the chance. He headed down the steps, his boots clomping heavily, suddenly in a hurry to put some space between himself and this woman. She had no idea what she did to him, that much was obvious.

And he wanted to keep it that way.

When he reached the kitchen, Bette was setting out the coffee cups. Aaron pulled out a chair and sat. He exhaled in relief, feeling as though he'd just made a narrow escape. From what, he wasn't entirely sure.

Riley came into the kitchen and pulled out another chair.

"That was quick," Bette said.

"I'll unpack later," Riley told her. She shed her parka and draped it over the back of another chair.

As Aaron had suspected, she was nicely put together, with soft curves in all the right places and a tantalizing little rear packed into form-fitting jeans. He could appreciate it here, in the safety of the kitchen.

Bette poured three cups of coffee, and said, "I'm all out of that creamer you like, Aaron."

"Don't worry about it," he told her. "I can't stay long anyway. I've been gone from the restaurant for a week. I want to get back and see how things've been getting along without me. I have a new manager. This is the first time I've left her in charge for more than a couple of days."

"I heard you gave that job to Virgie Marks," Bette said, setting the cups on the table. "That was generous of you, considering the history there."

Aaron wrapped his hands around his cup and shrugged. "She's working out fine for me so far."

Standing beside the refrigerator, Riley looked over at Aaron. "What kind of history?" she asked.

He glanced up at her, eyes narrowed. "Virgie used to own the restaurant I bought." He downed half of his hot coffee in one swig, set his cup on the table with a clatter and stood. This wasn't the direction he'd wanted the conversation to go. "Thanks for the coffee, Bette. See you around, Red."

He walked out of the kitchen without looking back at them.

"Well!" Riley huffed. "That was sudden. First he sticks like glue and I can't shake him, then he just gets up and walks out."

"I think Aaron has taken more heat for buying some of the foreclosed properties around here than he likes to let on," Bette explained. "Virgie opened the restaurant a few years ago, when real estate was high and the economy was booming. When things began to slow down she couldn't keep up with her payments, and she lost the place."

"It's happening all over," Riley said.

"It sure is. Three businesses on Main Street have closed in the past year. Aaron moved in and bought a couple of places, the restaurant being the first. He's also bought some houses."

"All at other people's expense."

"That's not his fault."

"But he's taking advantage of it." Riley crossed her arms and sat back. She knew the type. She dealt with dozens of businesses and business owners in her line of work. She'd seen many businesses fold, and she'd witnessed firsthand the devastation it could cause. Not just to the business owners, but to their families as well.

And she was well aware of the speculators who swooped in during hard times and bought someone else's dream for pennies on the dollar.

"Aaron didn't have to give Virgie a job as manager of the restaurant," Bette said. "He was doing her a favor."

Riley snorted. "Some favor. She'd be better off finding something else. Now she just has to go there every day and be reminded of what she lost."

Bette wagged a finger at her. "Virgie could have turned down the job offer when Aaron made it. She took it because he's paying her a decent wage, which allows her to stay here near her family. Don't be so quick to judge, young lady, when you don't know the whole story."

"Sorry," Riley said, chastened. "How's the restaurant doing since he took over?"

"Better than ever."

"Somehow, that doesn't surprise me," Riley said.

In the short time she'd been around him, Aaron had oozed confidence, a trait that would undoubtedly carry him well in any and all business ventures.

And, since he'd gone, the vitality-level in the kitchen had definitely decreased. As irritating as he'd been, he'd added a spark to the surroundings.

In a corner of the kitchen Riley spotted her grandmother's computer, the one she'd taken great pride in buying several years ago.

Riley got up and went to it. "This thing could probably use some updating."

"Oh, I'm not sure I'd bother," Bette said. "I just use it mainly for my genealogy work. I've joined a club, did I tell you? I'm researching our family tree."

"What about your bookwork for the resort? Aren't all your files in there?" She tapped a couple of keys. The screen remained dark. She pushed the button on the tower, which sat next to the monitor, and waited. Nothing happened. "Are you having trouble with this?"

Bette stood at the sink. "I haven't been on in a couple of days, but it was fine last time I looked," she said.

Riley pulled the tower away from the wall. All the cables were properly connected. She got down on her knees and peered underneath, following the cables and wires that went from the computer to the power surge protector on the floor. Everything there was properly connected, but the surge protector was not plugged into the wall. She plugged it in, and came back up.

She pushed the button on the tower again. A little green light blinked, accompanied by the welcome hum of a computer coming to life.

Bette rinsed out their coffee cups. "Aaron's restaurant is one of the best in the area," she said. "There was even a write-up about it in the *Sioux City Journal* a few months back. He's worked hard to make it what it is, and the food's good. You should see it while you're here."

"He invited me. I'll go if you'll come with me." Riley examined the icons on the computer's desktop, found the one for the resort's bookkeeping records and double-clicked.

Riley's eyes stayed on the computer screen. Her grandmother's bookkeeping records were not current. "What about here?" she asked cautiously. "How's business doing?"

With her eyes turned to something outside the kitchen window, Bette's voice barely rose above a whisper. "It's not the same without your grandfather."

"I know it's not, Gran, but it's not like that just happened," Riley said gently. "You've been keeping up with things by yourself for the past few years."

"It gets harder every year." Bette managed a smile. "It's so good to have you home."

There was that word again—home.

"It's good to be back," Riley said, deciding not to argue the point. She went to the kitchen window and, standing beside her grandmother, pulled the curtain back to look out.

The lake's surface, frozen over now, was dotted with ice shacks. The lake was so wide that the other side wasn't visible from here, and an excursion around it would easily take an hour.

"I've never seen the lake like this," Riley said of the silver and white view. "I didn't know it was so pretty in the winter. It's like a picture postcard. But I don't think I could take the cold for very long."

"You get used to it," Bette said. "Besides, there's a real charm to seeing the change of seasons in all their glory."

Riley let the curtain drop. She told her grandmother about running into Lauren at the coffee shop, and her surprise at seeing her old friend after all these years. "She didn't get far from town, did she? When we were kids Lauren was so full of plans. She wanted to see the world."

"Life has a way of changing one's plans," Bette said. "Lauren did move away for a couple of years, but she came back. Then she got married and had a couple of kids, and got divorced. Now she's raising her children by herself, and I imagine she finds that easier to do here, near her family. I've always liked Lauren. She's a good kid."

Riley smiled. "She's not exactly a kid any more. For that matter, neither am I."

"You'll both always be little girls to me."

Her grandmother filled Riley in on more local happenings, the weather—a warm front was predicted to be coming through—and a quilt shop in town that she liked. They talked about the cabins, then decided to go out and take a look at the units.

Finding an extra pair of her grandmother's boots in the front closet, Riley slipped her feet into them. Once outside, they walked the short distance to the cabins. Again Riley was struck by how they'd deteriorated since she'd seen them last. After unlocking Great Blue Heron, the cabin nearest the house, Bette pushed hard on the door, which groaned and moved reluctantly on rusted hinges.

The interior was even worse, and Riley bit back an exclamation of dismay. The cabins all followed the same floor plan—one open room that contained the main living area and the kitchen, with a tiny bedroom off to the side and an even tinier bathroom next to that. In the front room of Great Blue Heron the cushions of the sofa were worn to the point of showing stuffing in spots. A kitchen chair was tipped over on its side and had one broken leg that hung like the limb of an injured animal, and the wood floor was water-stained and warped.

Bette simply picked up the chair and leaned it against the Formica-topped table. "People leave things such a mess," she said. "Every year the guests are more inconsiderate."

"Your last guests left five months ago," Riley pointed out. "Didn't you clean the cabins out at the end of the season?"

"Five months? It hasn't been that long, has it?"

With a feeling of dread, Riley opened the door to the little bedroom. It was just as bad. There was a cold draft, and she found the window ajar. Pulling it shut, she thought of the water pipes. "Did you drain the pipes in the fall?" she asked anxiously.

"Of course," Bette said, indignant. "They'd freeze otherwise."

Before they left Riley made sure the cabin was secure, but she didn't have a good feeling about any of this.

Back inside the house again, Riley went upstairs and unpacked. This was the room she'd always stayed in when she was a kid, with its window overlooking the lake.

At one time this little room had been one of her favorite places on earth.

That had changed. She knew exactly when—at the time of her parents' divorce. Caught up in the ugliness of that particular situation, Riley and her sister had been victims of the ensuing bitterness. It had left them both with emotional scars.

Meghan had married young in an effort to recapture the family life she craved. Fortunately, it had worked out well for her. She had a good marriage.

Riley, on the other hand, had gone in the opposite direction. Though she'd had a couple of long-term relationships over the years, she'd never trusted enough to really give of herself to another person. There was a part of herself she kept, out of a sense of self-preservation, shut away.

It was the only way to keep from getting hurt.

She set her laptop up on the desk and turned it on, thanks to the wireless network card and network server of the company she worked for. There were several ongoing projects she needed to keep an eye on, even while she was away from the office, projects that involved clients she'd brought to the company, and whose websites were in varying stages of completion. This really hadn't been a good time for her to leave for several days. To get the needed time off she'd promised Emily Rosa, vice president of the company and her boss, that she would continue her work on her laptop while in Iowa.

Riley caught up with a few things, answered some e-mails, checked sites. After a while, she turned away from the laptop, rubbing her eyes.

She went back downstairs and entered the kitchen just as the phone was ringing. Her grandmother answered it, then held the cordless phone out to Riley. "It's for you," Bette said.

"Me?" Eyebrows lifted in surprise, Riley took the receiver. If anyone from work wanted to reach her, they'd e-mail or call her cell phone.

It was Lauren, already wanting to know how the visit was going. Riley refrained from pointing out that she'd only been here a few hours. It was actually good to hear Lauren's voice.

"It feels weird to be back in my old room," Riley said, leaning back on the chair. "My grandmother hasn't changed a thing. It's like a time capsule."

"Tell me about it," Lauren said. "After my divorce I moved back in with my folks for a few months while I got back on my feet. Me *and* my two kids jammed in my old bedroom, complete with my Culture Club posters still on the walls."

Riley laughed. "I remember your posters. You were also big on Madonna."

"Hey, Madonna still rocks."

Lauren filled her in on people she'd all but forgotten, and Riley was quickly caught up in the nostalgia-inducing conversation as one name led to the memory of another.

"There've been a lot of changes around the lake since I was here last," Riley said after a while.

"I get all the latest news at the Kozy Korner. That place is a hotbed of gossip and information, especially this time of year when the locals don't have much more to do than meet for coffee and swap stories. I hear about the latest family to move away, who's having money problems and which kids are causing their folks the most grief."

Lauren also touched briefly on her failed marriage, but didn't dwell on it. Finally, because they seemed to still have so much to talk about, she suggested they get together.

"It's not all bad," she said. "I can show you some of the town. We could go to Aaron's restaurant. It has a bar attached, with a little dance floor and a jukebox, but it's not a rowdy place. We can sit and chat."

Aaron's restaurant. With those words Riley experienced a little thrill of anticipation, and she had a vivid mental image of his face looming close to hers in the upstairs bedroom.

It was probably a sad testament to the state of her love life, which was currently suffering through a long dry spell that was undoubtedly making her vulnerable. With his casual manner and lopsided grin that seemed to mock even as it charmed, the mere mention of Aaron Wolfe had caused stirrings that were catching Riley totally off guard.

But she had to keep her priorities in order.

"No, I'm not going out my first night here," she said. "I'm going to stay and visit with my grandmother."

"Oh, sure," Lauren said. "I should've thought of that. We'll do it another time."

Bette, a few feet away, was gesturing at Riley. Riley put one hand over the mouthpiece and looked at her.

"Go," Bette said, waving her hands in a *shoo-ing* motion.

"No," Riley said. "I'm here to see you. I'll go out another night."

"You should see your friends."

"I don't have 'friends' here. Just Lauren, and she understands."

"I understand," Lauren's voice said, coming out small through the earpiece of the phone.   "Go," Bette persisted. "I'll be in bed in a couple of hours anyway. You won't even have to climb out the bedroom window this time."

Riley choked back laughter. "I never—"

"Busted," Lauren's voice came through.

"I insist," Bette said firmly. She *shoo-ed* again, and looked determined to drive Riley from the house for the evening.

Riley sighed. She was losing this battle. "Maybe just for a while."

"Good," Bette said.

"Great!" Lauren said. "I'll pick you up at nine."

"Do you live close?"

"Practically around the corner," Lauren said.

At the appointed time, Riley opened the front door for Lauren. She'd run a brush through her hair and put on a little lipstick, and in her grandmother's comfortable boots again she felt considerably steadier on her feet as she followed Lauren out to her car.

Bette stood on the front porch and waved to them as Lauren backed her car out of the driveway.

"So, she knew all along about the time you shimmied down the drainpipe on the side of the house when we were thirteen," Lauren said. "And she never said anything to you before now?"

"Not a word," Riley said.

They both smiled and waved one last time at Bette before Lauren turned the car onto the road and sped away.

"Of course, I didn't really perfect my sneaking-out skills till a couple of years later," Riley added.

Lauren drove fast, but she maneuvered around the curves with the skill of a long-time resident. "Y'know, we don't have to go to Aaron's if you don't want. There are a few other places open in town, even this time of year."

"No, I don't mind going to Aaron's," Riley said casually.

Not casually enough, apparently, because Lauren cut her a sharp sideways glance. "Yeah, he's something, isn't he? I might've been interested myself if things were different."

"Different how?" Riley asked.

"Divorced with two kids."

"Aaron?" Riley asked, startled. Her grandmother had said nothing about that.

"No, silly—me," Lauren laughed. "Between work and keeping track of my kids, I have all I can handle right now."

"Well. . . I'm not interested in him," Riley said.

"Here we are," Lauren said cheerily.

She'd careened around one last corner and the restaurant came into view. The parking lot was half full, and through the front windows they could see an expanse of cloth-covered tables, and waiters and waitresses moving efficiently about.

Lauren parked, and Riley followed her to the building. She wondered if Aaron would be around or, as the owner of the establishment, he would rule from afar. It'd been months since she'd been in a bar. Back home her social life tended to revolve around company gatherings and client meetings, with the occasional convention thrown in. A typical night consisted of flipping through the latest web-graphics catalogs, usually in her pajamas, with a CD playing in the background and, if she was feeling really festive, maybe a single glass of wine.

God, she was pathetic.

THREE

When he looked up and saw Riley Harrison entering the bar, Aaron, in the process of pouring bourbon into a shot glass, missed. He quickly wiped up the mess.

Bartending was not his forte. He was more accustomed to the wheelings and dealings of real estate acquisitions than of actually running a restaurant. He liked finding properties he knew he could get at a bargain price, and then going in for the kill.

Purchasing the West Woods had been a particularly satisfying buy. The bank that had foreclosed on the property had been eager to sell. Aaron's intent had been to hang onto the business, wait until the market turned around again—which it always inevitably did—then sell it at a tidy profit.

What he hadn't expected was that he'd actually have to work the place himself to build it back up. He'd been surprised at the amount of resistance he'd encountered from the citizens of Lake Okoboji. He'd been unable to find anyone to run the restaurant, and had been forced to take over the task himself. For the better part of the past year, he'd been making himself known in the community, gaining trust, knocking down the walls of resistance.

Only recently had he begun to make some real headway. He'd gone to his cabin up north for a week to think about things, and to contemplate his next move.

Now, watching as Riley and Lauren took a table near the dance floor, Aaron was glad he'd come back when he had, glad he'd made that stop at the coffee shop, and especially glad that he'd gotten a haircut and shave before coming in to work tonight.

Angie, one of two waitresses working the bar for the

evening, approached with empty tray in hand, having just delivered the latest round of drinks to a group of partiers in the far corner.

"Couple of new ones just came in, Angie," Aaron said.

She turned and looked over her shoulder. "Who's that with Lauren?"

"Riley Harrison. She's Bette Harrison's granddaughter, here visiting for the week. From Texas."

Angie gave him a look from beneath her blue-striped bangs. "*Hmmm.* Interesting how you know all that already."

The interior of the bar was a pleasant surprise to Riley. There was a small dance floor off to one side, as Lauren had said, and of course the obligatory jukebox. The clientele consisted of a few couples sitting at tables, and several individuals on the barstools. There was also a mixed group of about a dozen people at one long table who looked to be celebrating something.

And there he was—Aaron Wolfe, behind the bar, talking to a cute waitress with neon hair. At least Riley *thought* it was him. The transformation since that afternoon was incredible. Gone was the shaggy, untamed-look of a few hours earlier. Since then he'd gotten a haircut, though it still curled a little behind his ears and touched the back of his collar. He'd also shaved, which was an improvement because he had a nicely squared jaw that was now shown to its fullest benefit, and his plain white shirt, open at the collar, revealed a tantalizing peek of brown chest hair.

"What's wrong?" Lauren asked as they took an empty table near the dance floor. "Your face is all flushed all of a sudden."

"Nothing. I'm fine. It's a little warm in here."

"It's not warm in here at all."

"Okay, so I'm having a hot flash. What can I say?" Riley looked away from the knowing mirth in Lauren's expression.

Then Aaron was at their table, and the hot flash upgraded to a two-alarm blaze.

"Hiya, Lauren. Red," he said.

"It's Riley," she said, letting her eyes travel up to meet his.

"I know it is. But I've always had a soft spot for red hair."

"Maybe the soft spot's in your head," she said before she could stop the words.

He laughed, showing all of his straight white teeth. Though Riley's cheeks burned, she refused to drop her gaze. He was intrusive, annoying and—go ahead, admit it—damn sexy. He seemed to see right into her, mocking her attempts to make sensible decisions about her life. But sensible could be synonymous with dull, and there was nothing dull in the tall figure that loomed over their table, nor in the feelings that hummed through her like unexpected electricity.

"What can I get for you ladies?" he asked.

Riley asked for white wine, Lauren the same, and Aaron left to get their drinks.

They watched him go, then heaved a joint sigh as he moved back around behind the bar.

"That's some nice scenery," Lauren said.

"Definitely," Riley agreed. "I work with men who sit at computers all day. None of them are built like that."

Aaron brought their drinks. Again they watched him go, and again they both sighed.

"Tell me about your kids," Riley said to Lauren, determined to regain control of this situation. "How old are they? What are they doing tonight?"

Lauren didn't fight the change of subject.

"Chloe's thirteen, and Jake is nine," she said, fingers on the stem of her glass. "Chloe's old enough now to watch her brother, but Jake doesn't always listen to his sister the way he did for a regular sitter, so I won't stay out late. Besides, it's a school night. I'll get them up early, then I'll go off to my job at the coffee shop. That's part-time. I also have a little antique shop in my garage, but this time of year I don't see much business."

"How do you do it all?"

"I manage. Organization is the key. The job at the coffee shop isn't glamorous, but it's an income, and I have enough flexibility that I can go to the kids' games and school events with a minimum of hassle."

"Don't you ever date?" Riley asked.

"Like I said, I don't have a lot of spare time. What about

you—anyone special back home to get you all heated up?"

"Not lately," Riley said. She didn't want to admit that it had been months since she'd had a real date. "My work keeps me busy, too."

"You said you design websites—so you must be on the computer a lot?"

"All day," Riley said. "I work for a marketing company that specializes in web design and hosting. When I need to I can work on my laptop at home, or long distance, like I'm doing here."

"It sounds kind of lonely," Lauren observed.

Riley blinked, not sure how to take that, yet she couldn't entirely deny it. "I have several new clients whose websites I'm developing at work, plus some freelance stuff, so I'm in contact with people all the time."

"But not face to face."

"Well, no."

"I like interacting with people," Lauren said.

The lights in the bar dimmed. Money was dropped in the jukebox, and the resulting blast of music was greeted by an appreciative whoop from the group at the long table. A woman at the head of the table wore a silly party hat proudly, and a pitcher of frothy beer was being passed around and poured into upheld glasses.

A few people from the table got up and went to the dance floor, including the woman in her party hat. The music was medium tempo, and the couples swung each other about with happy abandon and little regard for actual rhythm. Riley had to smile, especially when Lauren lifted her hands over her head to clap her approval.

Without quite knowing how it'd happened, Riley had a second glass of wine in front of her and she was feeling more relaxed. The music changed to something slower, and several more people went out onto the dance floor. The bar was now half-full, the lights dimmer.

A hand touched her shoulder. Riley looked up.

Aaron leaned over, lips close to her ear, and whispered, "Dance with me."

His nearness sent a jolt of renewed voltage through Riley.

So far she'd managed to keep her attention on Lauren, but that flew out the window with the touch of Aaron's warm breath on her ear.

She started to shake her head, but Lauren said, "Go," and Aaron took her hand and pulled her easily to her feet.

Riley found herself on the dance floor, with Aaron's arm around her waist and her right hand engulfed in his. The top of her head barely reached his shoulder. She had a close-up view of the opening at the top of his shirt, and the indentation at the base of his throat where the pulse of his heartbeat seemed to keep time with her own.

"I was glad to see you come in the door tonight, Red," Aaron said.

"It was Lauren's idea."

The nickname didn't seem to annoy her as much this time, and she didn't bother to correct him. Besides, there was no cruelty there when Aaron said it, as there had been in those long-ago taunts by mean school kids. Coming from his lips the word was almost a caress, like the light brush of fingertips on receptive skin, and Riley felt a little woozy.

There were more people on the dance floor, so many now that he had to hold her close to keep her from being bumped. Or maybe he was holding her close because he wanted to, and she relaxed into the curve of his arm, fitting there so perfectly that it seemed they'd been dancing together for longer than just this few minutes.

And he smelled good. Not overwhelmed by aftershave, but natural, like autumn leaves deep in the woods after a rain— primal and of the earth.

It had to be the wine. It was affecting her in strange ways. Riley pulled back, her cheeks burning at the feverish thoughts that kept creeping into her head.

"What's wrong?" Aaron asked, his arm tightening around her.

She resisted the embrace, trying to keep a space of at least a couple of inches between them, or to at least keep her breasts from pressing against his chest. "Nothing," she murmured. She looked over at the couple dancing next to them, at the jukebox, anywhere except up at him. "It's warm in here, that's all."

His lips brushed her hair. "More than warm. I'd say it's hot."

Hot. Yes, it was that, and Riley wanted nothing more than to relax and let the heat surround them both and melt her reserves down to nothing.

She fought the urge with an iron will developed over years of practice. She had to maintain control, of herself if nothing else. Without it she was in peril of backsliding into dangerous territory. But it felt so good to dance, for the first time in she couldn't remember how long.

The song ended, leaving Riley with a sense of almost postcoital lethargy. A few of the couples on the dance floor drifted away, but before Riley could move to do the same Aaron pulled her in close to him, his arm strong and encircling, his hand tightening on hers. Not too much, just enough pressure to keep it pinned there in his palm.

"There's another song coming up," he said.

"I should . . ."

"Should what?"

Riley wasn't sure, but there was something she should do. Run for her life? No, that wasn't it. Get back to Lauren? Yes. She'd left Lauren alone at the table, and that was rude.

The music started again, another slow song. She looked over at the table. Lauren was still there, but she was talking to a bespectacled, slightly balding man who stood beside their table, drink in hand.

"She's fine," Aaron said, bringing her attention back to him. "A week isn't much time for us to get to know each other. I'll have to work extra hard while you're here."

The music, pulsating, surrounded them.

"I'm going to be spending all of my time with my grandmother," Riley said. "She's the reason I'm here."

"You need time to yourself, too. She'd want that."

"How do you know what my grandmother would want?"

"I'll bet I've seen more of Bette this past year than you have, so I know her pretty well."

Riley was taken aback at the implied accusation. "We've kept in close touch."

"I'm sure you have. But you live a long ways away, and I'm

right here where I run into her at the grocery store, at the post office, one place or another at least a couple of times a week." He looked down at her. "All I'm saying, Red, is that I think she'd want you to have a good time while you're here, and the two of you can't spend the whole week looking at each other over the kitchen table. You'll have to get out once in a while. The Winter Games festival is this week, bring her to that."

"The what?"

"It's a yearly event. Mostly a chance for people in town to get together and have a good time. There'll be a bonfire, games like broom-hockey and cross-country ski races. She's come in the past, so I know she enjoys it." His arm tightened again. "And I'd like to see you there."

The second song ended, and this time Riley did step back before he could pull her in again.

"I'll talk to her about it," she said.

Aaron walked Riley to the table, then went back to his place behind the bar.

Angie, who'd taken over pouring drinks while he was gone, picked up her tray and went back out onto the floor.

A half-smile formed on Aaron's lips as he washed some glasses. From back here he could watch Riley Harrison without being too obvious about it. It was good to have someone new in town, even if temporarily. He'd come to know most of the people in the area fairly well, but the disadvantage to that was there was little mystery left to spice things up. He knew Lauren worked hard to take care of her kids and received a measly child support from her ex. Angie, the waitress, was working two jobs to save money for college next fall, and couldn't wait to leave here and move to the city.

He poured drinks for a new group that came in and took a table near the bar, his eyes regularly drifting over to where Riley and Lauren sat.

He suspected Riley held some secrets, as most adults who'd lived at all did, and the flicker of rebellion that swept over her expressive face so easily intrigued him. She had no talent for hiding her emotions, though he suspected she didn't realize this. In a very short time he'd seen hints of stubbornness, independence, and a deep determination to do things her way.

Angie, appearing in his line of vision, set a glass down in front of him. "This was supposed to be a JD press, but you made a JD water."

He took the glass and set it on the sink. "Sorry," he said, amused by the way Riley Harrison had so invaded his thoughts that he was now messing up simple drink orders. "I'll make a new one."

"And don't let it happen again," Angie said, giving him a knowing look.

FOUR

Riley lay on the bed, her bare feet propped on the headboard, head hanging over the side of the mattress. The phone was pressed to her ear.

"It's nice to be back, especially in my old room," she said into the mouthpiece. She thought of it as more of her room than Meghan's, for, though Riley had visited regularly, Meghan had been prone to homesickness and had come only a few times. "You should see it, nothing has changed. I even found an old cotton windbreaker of mine in the closet. But it's too small now and moths or something got to it, so I threw it out."

"How is Gran doing?" Meghan asked. "I sent her pictures of the kids last month. Did she get them?"

"She got them, she said to tell you thanks. I'm going downstairs in a minute to help with breakfast, then I'll go through her paperwork. I looked at some of it yesterday, but I was out last night so I didn't get a chance to—"

"You went out last night?" Meghan interrupted. "You mean with Gran?"

Riley made a face, but it was too late to take back the words. "Well, no . . . not with Gran. With a friend from town."

Disapproval vibrated through the phone lines. "You went out with a friend on your very first night there? You just left Gran home alone?"

"She's been living alone for several years," Riley reminded her.

"Of course she has, so she's probably been looking forward to your visit. How could you run out on her like that? And who was this friend? What's his name?"

Sitting up on the bed, Riley crossed her legs. Her hair fell in her face and she pushed it back with an impatient hand. She

37

was determined not to let it get to her, but the pleasant glow she'd been feeling was nonetheless already fading.

The night before she'd come home to a silent house, dark except for the light in the entryway that her grandmother had left on for her, and had come upstairs to curl up in the big, comfortable bed that welcomed her like a long-lost friend. For once she hadn't worked at her computer far into the night, as was often her habit, but instead had fallen almost immediately into a deep, restful sleep.

"*Her* name is Lauren. We used to hang out together when we were kids. You remember, I used to write to her sometimes. Gran wanted me to go. She practically pushed me out the door."

"Oh, sure. Where did you go?"

"That's not important, and I was only out for about an hour." No way was she going to pour fuel on this fire by telling Meghan she and Lauren had gone to a bar.

"Still, I think—"

"I'm pretty sure I know what you think," Riley said. "You wanted me to let you know how things are going here, and I have. I have to go now. Give the kids a hug for me, and hi to Mike."

Riley hung up before her sister could say anything more. She continued to sit cross-legged, and tried a few deep-breathing exercises to clear her head. It wasn't like she'd been out all night. An hour or so, as she'd said, and she and Lauren hadn't danced on any tables or closed the place down. After the two brief dances with Aaron, she'd returned to the table where she and Lauren had chatted some more about their lives, their families, their work, then had decided to call it a night. It was surprising how quickly they'd slipped back into an easy camaraderie, as though the years in between amounted to nothing more than a blip in time.

Jumping up from the bed, Riley padded on bare feet to the bathroom.

When she entered the kitchen a short while later she was freshly showered and shampooed, her towel-dried hair damp on her shoulders, dressed in jeans and a big flannel shirt.

"Smells good," she said, giving her grandmother a hug.

Bette already had a robust breakfast of scrambled eggs, oatmeal and bacon prepared. Riley set the table, and as they ate she told her grandmother about her truly nice visit with Lauren the night before, and even admitted to dancing a little, though she didn't mention with whom she'd danced.

When they were finished eating, Bette said, "I usually go for a walk after breakfast."

"I'll go with you if you'll give me a few minutes to check in at work."

Riley went upstairs, sat at her laptop and checked a few of her ongoing projects. When she noticed that some of the pictures in one of her newly developed sites looked grainy, she used her cell phone to call work.

"Joel," she said, putting the tiny instrument on speakerphone to free up her hands, "I'm looking at the Freemantle Accounting web pages. What's happened to those images?"

Joel, two thousand miles away, said, "Give me a second. Okay, there it is. What's wrong?"

Tapping at the keys on her laptop, Riley went to the company's shared drive, but found her access denied. "Damn," she muttered. "I can't get in. Open up one of the images and check the resolution. It must be too low. The pictures were good to start with, so the distortion must have happened in the transfer."

Riley checked more pages on her laptop, frowning at what she saw. She would settle for nothing less than perfection, and these images were far from that.

"You should be here for this, Riley," Joel said. "It's your account, and you know whatever happens, Emily will hold you responsible."

"I know," she sighed. Their boss was even more of a perfectionist than Riley. The Freemantle Accounting site was a major client that Riley had snagged a month earlier, and she'd worked to get everything up and ready to go before leaving the office for this trip. "I'll have to take a look at it later. See what you can do on your end."

Riley pushed her feet into her grandmother's Docs again,

laced them up and headed downstairs. Expecting to find her grandmother waiting for her, she instead found the house empty and the front door wide open, cool air flowing into the exposed front rooms. She put on her red parka and stepped out onto the front porch, pulling the door closed behind her as she called out, "Gran?"

No answer. With the parka unzipped, she walked out into the yard.

"Gran?"

"Over here."

Relieved, Riley trotted toward the cabins. She found her grandmother stooped at a rock-encircled flowerbed, pulling dried brown shoots from the frozen earth.

"I might plant petunias here in the spring," Bette said as she straightened, brushing the dirt from her hands.

"That would be nice. Did you know you left the front door open?"

"Did I? I'd better take care of that." Bette moved as though to go back to the house, but Riley put a hand on her arm.

"It's okay, I closed it."

Bette looked down at the flowerbed again. "We should be able to put about a dozen petunia plants in here. You have a good eye for design, I'll let you choose the colors."

"Gran, I won't be here in the spring," Riley said carefully. What was going on here? A chill that had nothing to do with the weather ran through her.

"You won't? Oh, of course not." Bette smiled at her. "What was I thinking?"

"Where are your glasses? Do you want to get them before we go for our walk?"

Bette lifted a gloved hand to her face as though surprised to discover she wasn't wearing her glasses. "I must have left them inside. No, I don't need them right now, I use them mostly for reading and when I'm on the computer."

Hooking her arm through her grandmother's, Riley said, "Let's go for that walk then. I could use the exercise after that huge breakfast. Bacon *and* oatmeal? How do you keep your figure, eating like that every day? I'd be rolling through here like a tank."

"I don't eat like that every day. I cooked more than usual for you."

"Oh, thanks. We'd better walk."

Together they strolled down to the snow-covered beach, and to the resort's dock, which stretched out twenty feet over the frozen lake. With the vast expanse of ice and the ice shacks far out near the center, the lake had a peaceful beauty. Morning sunlight on the ice sparkled like a million tiny diamonds, reflecting pale colors that shimmered with the slightest movement of air along the surface.

The walk seemed to revive Bette. A dog barked somewhere nearby, and beyond that was a low buzzing sound, like a large, angry insect. Along this stretch of shoreline the houses were set farther apart than in other areas around the lake. The land here was at a premium, and valued for the thick woods beyond each back door, as well as the fine texture of the sandy beach during the summer months. The lakeshore houses here tended to be large, with deep yards and private docks. The dock for the resort was wider and extended farther out onto the lake that its neighbors', the extra size being needed to accommodate the boats, canoes and jet-skis that the guests at the resort often rented during their stay.

The buzzing sounded again, louder this time, and Riley looked back at the wooded area behind the houses.

"A snowmobile," Bette said, seeing her puzzlement. "They're all over the place this time of year, usually on that trail that goes all the way around the lake. They reached the dock but didn't venture out. It looked slick. They heard barking again, and then a scruffy white dog was bounding toward them. Riley instinctively stepped in front of her grandmother, even though the animal's tail was wagging with apparent friendliness.

"That's Kirby," Bette said.

The dog reached them and stopped, tongue hanging out, rear wiggling enthusiastically. He came only to about Riley's knees, and by his short legs and thick coat, she guessed he was a floppy-eared terrier mix.

"Hi, Kirby." Bette bent and patted the little dog's head.

"Kirby! Get back here!"

The dog's ears drooped and he turned to look at the male voice that commanded. Bette stiffened, and her eyes narrowed at the approaching figure.

The man walking toward them was tall and lanky, his wrists hanging below the cuffs of his jacket as though he'd outgrown it, though he appeared to be in his late twenties. His boots crunched on the snow, and when he reached the dog he grab its collar and gave it a jerk. "Kirby, sit!"

The dog obeyed, but gave Bette and Riley one last, tentative wag of its tail.

"Hello, Duane," Bette said, her voice flat. "Duane Myron, this is my granddaughter, Riley Harrison. She's visiting."

Riley held out a hand to the man, but he ignored it with a dismissive shift of his eyes.

"Visiting for how long?" he asked Bette. "Does this mean there'll be cars coming and going all the time? I noticed there were quite a few yesterday."

Besides her own car, Riley could think of only two others that she knew of—Aaron Wolfe's and Lauren's.

"Duane, we've had this conversation," Bette said. "If you don't like the traffic, you shouldn't have bought a house next door to a summer resort. There are quieter areas around this lake you could have chosen."

"My mother and I like where we're at just fine. We're not going anywhere."

"Good for you. Neither am I."

The hostility between them was palpable. They looked like two duelists ready to begin battle. Then Duane shifted his gaze back to Riley, and he seemed to really see her for the first time. An internal struggle played over his sharp features, until finally he forced what might have passed for a friendly smile if it hadn't been for the hardness in his stare.

"Hey, I'm sorry." He held out his hand, and Riley took it reluctantly. "You're visiting here, you don't want to hear all this old crap. Your grandmother I have a friendly feud going on about all the noisy kids and boats and stuff during the summer. My mother and I prefer peace and quiet."

"I see." Riley retrieved her hand and resisted the urge to wipe it on her parka. To distract from the discomfort she felt, she reached down and stroked Kirby's head. "Nice dog."

Duane grabbed the dog's collar and pulled it out of her reach. "Don't get too close. He bites."

"He does?" Riley looked at the pooch, which seemed unable to suppress a friendly tongue-loll that made him appear to be grinning at her. "If he's so vicious, why is he running around loose?"

"He gets out sometimes. That's why I worry about the kids around here all summer. Kirby's protecting our property. We have that right, but these kids wander all up and down the beach and come into our yard like they think it's part of the package. Someone's going to get bit one of these days, and it won't be our fault."

"Dua-a-a-ne! Telephone."

The three humans and Kirby all looked toward the source of this new voice. A tall, middle-aged woman stood on the porch of the next house over. When she saw she had their attention, she lifted a hand in greeting. "How are you this morning, Bette?" she called out.

"C'mon, Kirby." Duane gave the dog another jerk, and together they walked toward the house at a brisk pace. He didn't glance back at Riley and Bette.

"I'm fine, Geneva. Thanks for asking," Bette replied, returning the wave. She lowered her hand and said, under her breath, "Bitch."

"Gran!" Riley stifled laughter.

Bette turned and started walking back toward her own house. Riley fell in step beside her.

"They moved in two years ago and all they've done since is complain," Bette said as they headed back to the house. "Too noisy in the summer, too much traffic because of the business, Frisbees thrown in their yard. In the winter they gripe when I run my snow-blower, and in the fall it's the leaves that blow into their yard. For a while raccoons were getting into their garbage because they aren't smart enough to put a rock on the lid, and they said my cat was doing it."

"You have a cat?"

"No. But that doesn't stop them. They're the worst neighbors I've ever had, and if you ask me there's something peculiar about a man his age who still lives with his mother, though she's full of excuses for him."

They reached the front porch of the house.

"Are you going in already?" Riley asked. They'd hardly walked at all.

"I guess I'm not much in the mood to walk anymore. You go ahead if you want."

"You're sure you don't mind?" Riley felt the need for some physical exercise to rev up her metabolism. "I won't be gone long."

After insisting she'd be fine, Bette went inside the house. Riley turned and, parka still open, headed for the old hiking trail just behind the property line. There, feeling a comfortable strain in her legs, she picked up the pace. This was good exercise, better than just power-walking back home, because with the added weight of the boots and parka she'd get a real workout. The trail had an appealing arch of branches overhead that created a canopy through which the overhead sky peeked.

As she walked along the trail, the distance between the houses increased, and the trees around them grew thicker. After walking for several minutes, Riley noticed that the houses had become smaller and less modernized, more like summer getaways than year-round homes. Many looked closed-up, with curtains drawn over dark windows.

Something small and furry scurried under the porch of a log cabin as she walked past, making Riley jump, and for the first time she realized what an isolated area she'd come to. Possibly a squirrel, or maybe a raccoon. Did they hibernate in the winter? She didn't know, but she didn't relish the idea of coming face to face with some animal whose slumber she'd disturbed.

Then she heard the buzzing again, not far away. A snowmobile, her grandmother had said.

The trail was well maintained, with wooden signs posted at intervals giving a location or reminding hikers not to litter. There was even the occasional rest area, and she sat on a bench at one of these, enjoying the peacefulness of the setting.

The peace was shattered moments later when a snowmobile rounded the corner of the trail and came straight toward Riley, its long black skis jutting ahead of it like aggressive pointers. Crouched atop this apparition was a figure dressed head-to-toe in a hunter green snowsuit, with a helmet and an opaque visor that covered the face. The driver's gloved hand on the throttle moved, and the machine slowed, angled away from her and skidded to a snow-scattering stop less than five feet from where she sat.

Riley, who'd held her breath as the machine made its swift approach, stared with wide, surprised eyes at this apparition, one hand on her chest as though to keep her heart from flying away.

The rider cut the engine and sat back. With both hands he pulled off the helmet. "Hi. Didn't mean to scare you," the man said, reasonably enough.

Riley straightened her spine. "You took me by surprise, that's all. I heard you in the distance, but I didn't know you were getting so close."

He appeared to be in his late thirties, with light brown hair trimmed short, and a mustache that drooped down over the sides of a wide mouth. He wore lace-up boots with the snowsuit, and there was a patch attached to the front left breast of the outfit: DNR.

"Clay Johansen," he said. He removed his gloves and held one hand out to her. "Department of Natural Resources."

DNR.

Riley shook his hand and introduced herself. His official title made her feel better about running into a stranger out in the middle of nowhere.

"Your grandmother is pretty excited about you being here," Clay Johansen said, leaning back on the snowmobile. "She told me you were coming a few days ago when I ran into her. I live several houses down on the lake, in the A-frame."

"What are you doing out here?" she asked.

"Working." He reached around behind him and pulled a small cooler from a compartment on the side of the snowmobile. Swinging one leg around, he set the cooler down on the ground and opened the lid.

Riley's curiosity took her in for a closer look. Inside the cooler were several small labeled bottles, a notebook, and an assortment of instruments.

He took out the notebook and opened it. "This time of year I'm mostly taking notes on any changes I see in the area. If I find a thawed patch of water I'll take samples, and I get soil and plant samples when possible." He held up a zipped baggy, inside of which were a few brown leaves and spindly stems. "We're having a problem with Eurasian water milfoil around here. It got in, and left unchecked it could crowd out the native water plants in the lake and ruin it. It's a problem all throughout the state."

"What causes it?" Riley asked.

"It's brought in from other lakes, usually on boat propellers. If a boater doesn't check the propellers and the bottom of his boat carefully, then comes here and puts the boat in this lake, the weed gets in and takes hold. Once in, it spreads fast, and if it gets thick enough it can clog an entire waterway. Some smaller lakes in the state have been devastated by it."

"Sounds serious."

"Very serious," he said. "The more boat traffic we get here, the worse the milfoil problem will get. I'd like to see this entire area restored to something closer to its natural state someday. The people who live here have to decide if that's what they want, but it won't happen as long as the tourist season continues to explode."

Though she was interested in what he was saying, Riley was also aware that she'd been gone longer than she'd intended. "I should get back," she said. "Gran's going to wonder what happened to me."

He put the cooler back in the carrier. "Hop on, I'll give you a ride."

"On that?"

"Sure." He swung a leg over and got back on the machine, then scooted forward to make room for her behind him. "It'll be faster. And it'll definitely be more fun."

Riley stepped closer to peer dubiously at the machine. "I suppose it's like a motorcycle. I've been on a few motorcycles." Oh, yeah. In her rebellious youth.

"This is better. Trust me." He turned the key in the ignition and the snowmobile roared to powerful life, impatient to surge forward.

"Well . . . okay." She got on behind him and he handed her the helmet. "What about you?" she asked, taking it.

"I'll be fine."

Tucking her hair up, Riley put the helmet on her head. The visor dropped down, and she was immediately in a muffled world in which she could hear her own breath loud in her ears.

"Ready?" he asked over his shoulder.

She wrapped her arms around his waist. "Ready!"

The first surge forward caught Riley by surprise, and she tightened her grip on him. Sure, she'd been on motorcycles before, but that had been years ago and this was nothing like it. Closer to the ground, the snowmobile bucked with the first thrust, the skis taking the icy trail easily and with a speed that surprised her. Exhilarated and maybe just a little alarmed, she hung on.

Expecting him to stay on the trail, Riley was further surprised when Clay veered through an opening in the trees and rode out onto the lake itself. "Hey!" she yelped, but she was also laughing as the snowmobile shot across the ice with incredible speed. It felt as though they were flying, with fine crystals of snow pluming up several feet on either side.

Clay drove in the direction of her grandmother's house, then turned away from the curve of the shoreline, toward the center of the lake.

"Is this safe? Is the ice thick enough?" she yelled over the drone of the engine. Her voice, contained by the helmet, was loud in her own ears.

"It's thick enough to hold us in most spots," he yelled back over his shoulder.

She hugged him more tightly. "I don't find that reassuring."

He gunned the engine again and angled the machine to the right, turning sharply so it tilted, and the skis on one side came up a few inches off the ice. There were snowdrifts scattered about here. Clay headed straight for one and rammed into it. The snowmobile rose in the air about two feet, hitting the ice again with a padded thud that shook the machine and its passengers.

Riley squealed with delight. It was all so fast, there was no time to think about it or be really afraid. It was like being on a roller coaster, a breathtaking ride of speed and wind.

"You okay?" Clay hollered.

"I'm great!"

He circled one of the low snowdrifts, gunned the engine and took it again. For a moment they were flying, then they hit the ice with a bone-jarring thump that she felt all the way up her spine.

"Time to get back?" Clay asked after a moment.

"Yeah, I better," she agreed reluctantly.

Adjusting the throttle, he brought the speed of the machine down, and with that the noise level lowered considerably. He pointed off to their left. "Over there, see the dark spots on the surface? That's where the ice is thin. We won't go there."

"Oh, good. I'm glad to hear that."

He turned again, and the resort loomed ahead, drawing near. "You're safe," he said. "I know this lake better than anyone, and I've been riding my snowmobiles on it since I was ten."

He turned the machine so they headed toward the shore. They were within fifty yards of the resort's dock now, and there was a familiar SUV parked in front of the house.

"Looks like you have company," Clay said.

"Aaron. I wonder what he wants." But Riley felt a little lurch of anticipation, and her arms involuntarily tightened again around Clay.

He brought the snowmobile to a stop at the shore-end of the dock. Clay got up first, then reached down and pulled Riley to her feet. She wobbled unsteadily for a moment and he held her until she felt secure. "You've been here a day and you already know Aaron Wolfe?" he asked.

"We've met." She removed the helmet. Her hair fell to her shoulders. "Thanks for the ride. That was fun."

Clay looked like he wanted so say more, but he only took the helmet and put it on his own head. "You're welcome. Nice meeting you."

He hopped on the snowmobile, revved the throttle with a turn of his wrist, and shot out onto the ice, back in the direction from which they'd come.

Riley turned and walked toward the house, to where Aaron Wolfe waited for her.

FIVE

Standing beside his SUV, Aaron watched as Riley walked toward the house. He'd heard the snowmobile, had seen it soaring across the ice in this direction. At first he'd barely given it a glance, but then the red parka the passenger was wearing had caught his attention. *No, it can't be*, he'd thought. But it was. When Riley had removed the helmet and her auburn hair tumbled free, Aaron's jaw had hardened as he'd watched her with Clay Johansen.

He reminded himself of his reason for being here.

"You have a lot of free time on your hands for a businessman," Riley said when she was close enough. She looked over at the house. The front door was closed, and all seemed peaceful.

Aaron regarded her with interest. Dressed more casually now in jeans and a loose shirt that didn't hide her curves, she could pass for a local. It was a nice look on her, more relaxed, less the uptight city woman. "Not really, but I make time for what's important," he said. "Looks like you've made a new friend."

"I seem to be meeting people left and right. Everyone around here knows my grandmother, so that helps. What are you doing here?"

"Waiting for you. I wanted to talk to you about Bette. I think it's a good thing you're here, because I've been concerned about her lately."

Her eyes widened, and she tilted back to look up at him.

He continued, "I'm not sure she's up to running this place by herself any more. Not alone, anyway. You should consider sticking around."

"I'm here for a week," she said. "I can't just drop everything and stay. I have a job and a life to get back to in

Dallas. And my sister and mother are there."

"No boyfriend?"

"That's none of your business," Riley snapped.

"No husband, I know that."

"Again, none of your business."

"Everything is everyone's business around here," he said. Then he leaned down, his expression serious. "Riley, I didn't drive over here just to butt into your personal life. I was at the county recorder's office when your grandmother came in. She thought it was the post office. I put her back in her car and followed her home to make sure she got here okay. But she was confused, and I think she was a little scared."

She frowned. *"When* did this happen?"

"Just now. I've been here less than ten minutes, waiting for you to show up."

"Gran was in town? That's not possible, she's been home all morning." But Riley looked over at the garage attached to the house. The door was open, and the car inside was parked at an angle. "Oh, no," she said softly.

Aaron nodded, sympathetic.

"I'd better go in," she said. She hesitated, then added, "Thanks for seeing her home." .

"Think about what I said. This place is too much for her to take care of by herself. I know she's done it for years, but it's been getting harder for her. Last summer there were problems that I heard about. This is a small town at heart and word gets around. I heard there were some cases of double-bookings, where families showed up thinking they had a cabin rented, only to find there was nothing available for them."

"I can line her up with some additional summer help."

Riley started to walk away, but Aaron reached out and took her upper arm as he looked into her eyes. "I don't think that's going to be enough," he said.

"It'll have to be." Riley pulled her arm free and headed for the house.

Dreading what she would find there, Riley was pleasantly surprised to find her grandmother in her sewing room next to the kitchen, glasses perched on the end of her nose as she sorted through a wicker basket of fabrics. Her sturdy old Singer was in its usual place against one wall.

"How was your walk?" Bette asked, looking up from a folded length of cotton fabric.

"It was good. I met Clay Johansen, the DNR guy."

"Clay's a nice boy," Bette said, then smiled and held up a hand. "I know, he's not a boy."

Shedding her parka, Riley sat on the chair in front of the sewing machine. "I talked to Aaron, too," she said.

"Oh?" Bette held two swatches of fabric together, comparing them.

"He said you were in town, at the recorder's office."

Bette looked up. "Oh, that. The post office used to be next door to the recorder's office, till they built the new one a couple of years ago. Sometimes I get so busy thinking about what all I have to do that I forget to go to the new post office two blocks down."

"Is that all it was?" Riley asked, relieved. "Why didn't you wait for me to get back from my walk? I would've gone with you."

"I just needed some stamps, nothing to bother you about."

Relieved, Riley leaned back on the chair. Aaron had worried her over nothing.

After lunch they spent more time in the sewing room, then went to Bette's computer again, where Riley showed her some of the websites she'd designed.

"This one's for a seafood restaurant in San Antonio," Riley said, bringing up the home page. The colorful graphics boasted an animated lobster in the center of the screen.

Bette laughed as the lobster's claws opened and closed. "Oh, my."

"It's a little garish," Riley agreed, smiling along with her. "But it's what the client wants, and what the client wants is sacred."

They were playing with the lobster, clicking on its pincers to make the menu pop up, when there was a knock on the front door. After Bette's hollered, "Come on in!" Lauren and her children tumbled into the kitchen, filling it with noise and laughter. Chloe was tall for thirteen, all sharp elbows and coltish legs, but on her way to becoming lovely. Jake, nine, had freckles like his mother, and a shy smile. Lauren had just picked them up after school, she explained, and they were on their way to a craft show at the mall.

"You'll like it," she added. "Moose head coat racks, sweatshirts with snowmen embroidered on front. Kind of like the flea markets we used to go to in the summer, except inside."

"What do you feel like doing?" Riley asked her grandmother. She'd been watching her all day for signs of fatigue or confusion, and had seen nothing to cause concern.

"I never miss a craft show," Bette said. "I can look at fabrics there."

"I guess we're in," Riley said.

The mall was an enchanting arena of handmade quilts, woodcraft items, dolls and ceramics. There was a carnival atmosphere about the place, with long tables set up in every available space and people browsing, buying, or just hanging around and visiting with their neighbors.

"This is amazing," Riley said as they worked their way through the crowd. Chloe quickly found a group of girls her own age, and they formed a tight bundle of giggling energy that broke off and went in a different direction.

"Meet us at the front doors in an hour," Lauren called out to her daughter. To Riley she added, "That means in an hour and a half we'll have to go looking for her, and when I find her I'll be the bad guy for spoiling her fun."

Bette seemed to know everyone there. She introduced Riley to more people as they wound their way around tables, and browsed through upright bolts of fabric. Lauren stopped to look at some engraved redwood signs at the next table, while Jake charged on ahead, aiming for a display of handcrafted toys.

While her grandmother looked through fabrics, Riley approached Lauren. "Gran's having trouble keeping up with things by herself at the house, and with the cabins. I think she could use someone to come in and give her a hand. Do you know of anyone in town I can talk to about it?"

"Oh, sure," Lauren said. "I know a couple of women who do just that for the elderly, or for people who are busy and don't like doing housework themselves. I'll give you their names later."

"Thanks. I'll feel better when I go home if I know she has help." They walked over to a display of hanging quilts. Riley looked around, stood up on her toes and saw her grandmother two tables over, and relaxed. She also saw Duane Myron, who, when he caught her eye, raised a hand and flicked it by way of acknowledgment.

"Who's that?" Lauren asked.

"Don't you know him? He lives next door to my grandmother."

"Oh, yeah. Him and his mother, right? She's been in the coffee shop a couple of times, but they kind of keep to themselves."

Riley touched the hem of a particularly beautiful baby quilt. "This is nice. How much patience does it take to make something like this?"

"More than I have," Lauren said. "Oh, hi, Aaron."

Riley looked up and found that Aaron was, indeed, standing near them. Any earlier irritation she might have felt toward him vanished in this swift, surprising leap of delight.

"How're things going?" Aaron asked in a voice that was low, yet seemed to draw her in closer to him, which was his intent.

"Good," Riley said. "I asked Gran about this morning. She told me that the post office used to be next door to the building where you saw her, and she was just busy and forgot the new location."

He frowned, dark brows coming together between serious eyes. "I was there. She didn't just forget, she was confused."

"Well, she was fine when I got to her, and she's been fine all day. And I'm going to get some part-time help for her, with the house and the cabins. Lauren's going to give me some names."

He shook his head.

"What?" she asked defensively.

Aaron was shaking his head as much at himself as her. When he'd first met Riley he'd anticipated a few days of harmless mutual fun. Yet it seemed as though every time he was near her he had to bring up the subject of her grandmother, and their conversation turned somber.

"I don't think that'll do it," he said.

"Sure it will. She's fine most of the time, and if she has occasional lapses in memory—well, that's because she's getting older. It happens to all of us sooner or later."

Lauren had moved discreetly away and was talking to a man behind a table of yard ornaments, but there were still too many people around for Aaron to feel comfortable with this conversation. He would have preferred they go somewhere more private to talk, but Riley wasn't going to let it go. Her expressive eyes narrowed as she challenged him, and suddenly what he really wanted was to take her in his arms. He wanted to kiss those full lips and find out if they were as soft and tasty as they looked. He'd held her once already, when they'd danced, but it had been an exercise in frustration, just enough contact to whet his appetite for more and to keep him wondering about what lay beneath those bulky winter clothes.

Instead, he said, "You're going to get some stranger to come in a few hours a week and keep things in order for her?" His voice was deep with skepticism.

"Not some stranger," Riley pointed out. "Lauren will recommend someone, and you told me yourself everyone knows everyone around here. Why are you so interested, anyway?"

Lauren was working her way back toward them.

Aaron reached out and brushed Riley's cheek with the knuckle of his index finger. "I want to help."

She stepped back, and Aaron's hand fell to his side. "I don't need help," she said. "I have everything under control."

Lauren had almost reached them.

"I want to talk to you again," he said softly, his voice urgent. "I'll call you later." He waved at Lauren, then walked off in the opposite direction.

"He sure seems to be everywhere these days," Lauren said.

Riley watched him go. "Tell me about it. That's just what I need in my life—a pushy, almost-bankrupt restaurant owner giving me advice about my family."

They walked away from the quilts, and past a table of country-style pottery. They could see Bette and Jake not far ahead, and went in that direction.

"That's a little harsh," Lauren said.

Riley knew it was, but she felt confused and angry, and didn't know where else to direct her frustration. "It's true, isn't it?"

"Well, yeah, I guess that was the case awhile back," Lauren said. "But it wasn't his fault, and he's certainly proved himself since then. That man has a hand in so many different business projects around here I can't even keep track. Besides the restaurant, he owns a set of condos on the east side, and I heard he bought a boat-rental company last summer. I wouldn't even be surprised if he's interested in your grandmother's place."

"*What?*" Riley squeaked. She stopped walking so abruptly that a young mother with a toddler by the hand smacked into her back. Glaring, the woman went around them, pulling her protesting child along. "What do you mean by that?"

Lauren shrugged. "Just that he mentioned to me a few months back that he thinks the resort is a nice piece of property, and he wouldn't mind having something like it. That's all."

That's all. Riley turned this information over in her mind as they continued walking. She wasn't sure what to make of it, but there was one thing she was sure of—she was going to stay very much on her guard where Aaron Wolfe was concerned.

Bette purchased some fabric and new pinking shears at the mall, and once they'd located Chloe and dragged her reluctantly from her friends, Lauren dropped Riley and Bette off at home.

Riley helped take her grandmother's purchases into the sewing room. After a light supper, Bette was exhausted. Her earlier energy, perhaps too much to maintain, faded, and her face was etched with fatigue.

"Sit down, I'll take care of the cleanup," Riley insisted, taking their plates from the table. That Bette didn't argue the point spoke volumes. Riley filled the sink with soapy water, and put their few dishes in. "We can look through those fabrics of yours later and decide what to do with them."

"Tomorrow, maybe," Bette sighed. "I'm going to bed early tonight."

Again? Riley thought, but didn't say anything.

After the dishes were done and Bette had gone to her room, Riley went upstairs to her bedroom and sat at her computer. She looked at the problematic Freemantle Accounting site again and saw that the images there were still bad. She didn't like this forced dependence on others to get her work done. She always did things herself, even if it meant taking her work home with her. Oftentimes she'd get so caught up in what she was doing that she'd be at her computer well into the night, unaware of the passage of time.

Shutting down the computer, she leaned back in the chair and closed her eyes, going over the day in her mind. She was on sensory overload, trying to process all the new information that kept coming her way. And underneath it all was this undeniable attraction she felt for Aaron Wolfe, a fact she couldn't deny in light of her reaction every time she ran into the man. It was as though she'd been living in her work the way a canary lives in its cage, thinking that's the only world there is. Now, unexpectedly, the cage door had been opened and she could see there was something more and exciting out there, but she was still afraid to step through. The way out could be perilous, but having seen it, could she really stay timidly inside?

She thought about Aaron's touch on her cheek earlier, and the ripple of excitement it had sent through her. That light touch, combined with their two dances of the night before, was the most physical contact she'd had with a man in longer than she cared to remember. And there was so much more to Aaron than any of the men she'd met recently. She wasn't sure if he could be trusted, yet she felt herself drawn to him despite her efforts to drive him from her thoughts. She told herself to watch out for him, then melted when those eyes swept over her, mentally undressing—

The phone on the desk rang, and Riley jerked, startled, then grabbed for it before it could ring a second time and disturb her grandmother. She fumbled, dropped it, and picked it up again.

"I told you I'd call," Aaron said. "Can you come out and play?"

Her hand on the phone was sweaty. Did he somehow *know* when she was thinking about him? "Now?" she stammered.

"Sure. It's early."

She opened her mouth to say no, but somehow something else came out: "Are you at your restaurant?"

"No. I'm right outside."

"Outside where?" she asked, puzzled.

He laughed, the sound a deep rumble.

Something tapped against the bedroom window. Riley looked over at it, just in time to see a second pebble hit the glass with a *ting*. Pulling the corded princess phone with her, she went to the window and looked out. There, far below on her grandmother's front lawn, stood Aaron, his cell phone pressed to his ear.

Riley couldn't help it—she laughed. "You're crazy."

"Are you coming out or not?" he asked.

"Do you expect me to climb out the bedroom window? I gave that up years ago."

"I expect you to walk down the stairs, get your coat and come out the front door like a grownup."

She looked down at him and a smile spread across her face. What the hell.

"Give me a minute," she said, and hung up.

SIX

In the bathroom Riley checked her appearance, then ran a comb through her hair and brushed her teeth—the latter not because she had any big expectations, but because she'd had onions with supper.

She tiptoed down the stairs. In the kitchen she wrote a note to her grandmother, just in case, explaining that she'd gone out for a few minutes but would be back shortly. She left the note on the kitchen table, propped against the salt and pepper shakers.

After putting on her parka and boots, she went out the front door, closing it very softly behind her, and found Aaron waiting for her on the porch.

Riley whispered. "Do you always go around tossing rocks at windows in the middle of the night?"

"Only when it's someone I really want to see." He tilted his head toward his SUV, parked in the driveway. "Let's go for a ride. I want to show you something."

She hesitated. "No, I think I should stay here."

Aaron moved down one step. "She's asleep," he said, and held one hand out to her. "Please?"

That simple word won Riley over. If he'd insisted, or even attempted to be his usual pushy self, she'd already decided she would go right back inside. But because he was asking, and managing to do so very sweetly, she reached out and put her hand in his. His palm was warm, even without gloves, and she felt the strong heat enter her own skin and melt away the last of her reservations.

"Where are we going?" she asked, as they walked toward his SUV.

He gave her his most enigmatic smile. "It's not far. Nothing's far from anything around here. It's just something I think you'll enjoy seeing."

He opened the door for her and she slid into the front seat of his SUV. The interior was soft leather, and she leaned back comfortably as Aaron went around and got in on his side. He started the engine, and, without turning on the lights, backed slowly out of the driveway.

Riley again hadn't bothered to zip her parka. "It's funny," she said, "but I don't seem as bothered by the cold as I was at first."

"You get used to it. Spend a little more time here, and when the temperature gets above forty and the sun is shining you'll be running around in your shirtsleeves like everyone else."

"I doubt that."

"It's a fact. I spent a couple of years in Alaska, and in the spring when the weather started to turn I'd be outside playing soccer like everyone else, with no coat on—when it was a balmy ten above zero."

When the SUV was out of the driveway and facing away from the house, he turned on the headlights.

Riley laughed. "I don't believe you."

"It's true," he insisted. "After a few months of sixty below, ten above felt toasty."

She looked at his profile, backlit by the streetlights going by. "What were you doing in Alaska?"

"I was part-owner of a salmon fishing boat up there, and I helped run the excursions," he explained. "After a couple of years, I sold my share of the business and came back to Iowa."

"I've been wondering about something," Riley said.

He glanced over at her. "What's that?"

"When I first saw you yesterday, you had a beard and your hair was longer. Then, just a few hours later, you were a different person. Why the sudden change?"

"I have a cabin up north, and I'd been there for a few days," he told her. "I'd just gotten back. I hadn't even un-packed yet, and I sure hadn't had time to shave. As for the hair, I'd let it go for awhile, so I decided to go for a haircut and shave at the same time. You like?"

"It's an improvement. What do you do at your cabin?"

"This time of year it's mostly maintenance, and I like the peace and quiet of it. In the fall, though, I'll spend time up there for hunting season."

"What do you hunt?"

"Deer."

"You *kill* deer?" she asked, unable to hide her shock.

"Yes, Red, I do hunt deer," he said calmly. "Why the big surprise? I know Texans are hunters, and they do like their firearms."

"That doesn't mean I approve of it. And how can you hunt deer? They're harmless, beautiful creatures. Now, if it were a mountain lion, or something dangerous like that, I might understand."

"Spoken like a city girl," he said. "How much contact have you actually had with deer?"

He turned the SUV onto a side street.

"Well . . ." She thought about it. She'd taken her niece and nephew to a Sunday matinée of *Bambi* once, and of course there was the zoo, which they dragged her to at least once a year.

"That's what I thought," Aaron said.

He parked the SUV and turned to look at her, his arm across the back of her seat, the sleeve of his jacket brushing against her hair. "I agree with you that deer are beautiful creatures, but there are millions of them in this state alone. The roads are littered every spring and fall with carcasses of deer that have been hit by cars. They eat the crops and wander into backyards. They are not an endangered species, I hunt humanely, and I believe it's necessary to keep the deer population under control."

Riley thought hard for an argument to this, but couldn't come up with one that sounded strong enough. That they're pretty and remind her of Bambi just wasn't going to do it.

Aaron turned and looked out through the windshield. "This is what I wanted to show you."

She turned, and saw that they were parked at the entrance to an amusement park, a place that would normally be closed and dark this time of year but was now lit up against the night in a brilliant display of colored lights. The Ferris wheel was especially dazzling in all white lights, still and ghostly as it stood high above the park like a sentinel.

Aaron got out of the SUV, as did Riley. He came around and put a hand on her elbow, then guided her toward the park.

"Why is it like this?" she asked.

"I told you about the Winter Games," he said. "It's a festival held here at the park every February. The committee, which I'm on, has been working all week to get the park ready for tomorrow. Did you decide to bring your grandmother out for the activities?"

"I haven't asked her about it," she admitted. "But I will, in the morning."

"It starts in the early afternoon, with games and competitions. At sunset there's a bonfire."

"All of this is for one day?"

"It's a chance for people in the community to get together and have a little fun in a month when there's not much else going on. There's been talk of expanding it to two or three days starting next year, which I'm in favor of."

The ground had been sprinkled with rock salt to melt the ice, but Aaron still kept a protective hand on her arm as they walked. The iron front gates were closed and securely padlocked. They walked along the length of the heavy chain-link fence that surrounded the park, around to the beach side of the property. Overhead lights shimmered luminously on the ice-covered lake.

"It's wonderful," Riley said, enthralled by the sight. Without thinking about it, she slipped her hand into his. Their fingers entwined comfortably.

"I thought you'd like it," he said as they walked along the beach, away from the park. Within a few yards they reached an area where the beachfront homes began to show themselves. Their path was well-lighted by the security lights in most of the homes' yards, as well as by the dazzling, star-dotted sky overhead.

"And over there," Aaron said, indicating a three-story log house set well back from the beach and burrowed within a dense grove of tall trees, "is where I live."

Riley felt a chill run up her spine, but she didn't pull her hand from his. Instead, she looked up at him and said, "I'd like to see the inside."

In the moonlight Aaron's expression was unreadable. Without a word, still holding her hand, he led her to the house, where he opened the front door and turned on a light. He stepped aside so she could enter.

Riley looked around with interest. She'd wondered what kind of place Aaron lived in, but hadn't wanted to ask Lauren or her grandmother and give them more ammunition to tease her with.

The house was a pleasant surprise. Heavy oak furniture gleamed from a recent polishing, and smelled nicely of Lemon Pledge. It was a man's home to be sure, with no frills in the furnishings, very little on the walls and no knick-knacks that she could see. The overall effect was agreeably masculine and inviting, warm despite the monochromatic color scheme. But there were no mounted animal heads on the walls, for which she was grateful—*that* would've given her nightmares for a week. The front room was nearly as big as her whole apartment.

He followed her in and closed the front door.

"Your house is lovely," Riley said truthfully. "But isn't this a lot of space for one person?"

"It seems that way at times," he admitted. "C'mon, I'll show you the view."

They climbed an open stairway to the third level of the house, and there Aaron guided her through a set of sliding glass doors, out onto a balcony. Up this high the wind was sharp and biting. Riley zipped her parka, pulled the hood up and tucked her hands deep into the pockets.

But the view was astonishing, and within moments she hardly felt the cold.

The front side of his house faced the lake, and from the third story balcony they had a clear view of much of the lake in its entire frozen splendor, shimmering with a silent, ghostly radiance. The lights of the amusement park twinkled far to one side, and on the other side she could see a long stretch of curving beach, most of the homes set far enough back on their lots as to be almost hidden among the trees. The moon overhead was a white globe above the treetops, the stars incandescent witness to the scene below.

"Oh, Aaron, this is beautiful," she breathed. Tears came to her eyes. She tried to tell herself it was from the cold, and not the exquisiteness of the landscape below, but she was nonetheless surprised by her own reaction.

"Beautiful. Yes . . . it is," Aaron agreed, his eyes only on her. He stepped closer, gripped the hood of her parka on each side of her face, and gently turned her to him.

Looking up at him, Riley blinked back the tears that were like icicles on her lashes. She stood on her toes and lifted her face to him, and when his lips came down and covered hers the heat of his skin warmed her all the way to her long-frozen heart.

His lips were gentle and firmly insistent all at once. Aaron released her hood and his arms went all the way around her, pulling her close. It was similar to the dance they'd shared the night before, yet this was so much more. Riley wanted not to pull away from his embrace, but rather to meld herself to him, and the bulky multiple layers of their clothing were a hindrance to sudden, sweeping desire.

Aaron growled low, deep in his throat, the sound an echo of the one in her own head, and Riley's arms went around his waist to pull him closer to her, if that were possible. The ache of loneliness that had been a part of her for too long broke loose and began to dissolve, slowly, like a frozen pond in April that gave way reluctantly, in small increments.

He pulled back and Riley almost protested, would have if she'd been able to find her voice. But it was gone in breathless flight, and all she could do was allow him to hold her upright, for without his arms around her she would have collapsed in a boneless heap.

"You're shivering," he said, mistakenly believing it was the cold that made her tremble. "Let's go back inside."

Riley couldn't have objected if she'd wanted to, so she allowed him to lead her back into the house, and down two flights of stairs. In the spacious kitchen he propped her up against the sink and busied himself making two mugs of hot cocoa. She was still speechless, the blood roaring in her head.

"I forget how cold it can be up there if you're not used to it," he said, looking at her with concern as he mixed two packets of cocoa mix into mugs and placed them in the microwave. "I wanted you to see the view at night. Maybe I'm biased, but I think it's really something. The view was part of the reason I bought this house."

Finding her voice, Riley said, "I'm glad I saw it." She unzipped her parka, and resisted the urge to fan at her flushed cheeks with her hand.

She didn't know how to tell him she hadn't been cold, that she'd been kept warm by his arms, and by the kisses she'd wanted to never end. Up there on the balcony, it would have been so much easier to whisper in his ear how she felt, and she wished now she'd done just that. Here, in the brightly lighted kitchen, a sense of reality was returning, and the moment to reveal what was growing in her heart had passed.

The microwave *dinged*, and Aaron removed the mugs. Reaching high into a cupboard, he pulled out a bottle of peppermint schnapps and held it out with an inquiring tilt of his head.

"It'll warm you up," he said.

She nodded, and he poured a small amount of schnapps into each mug. He handed her one and she sipped, grateful for the liquid fire that slid down her throat and steadied her.

"The view up there is amazing," she said. "Your whole house is. It makes my apartment back home look like a closet."

Aaron went to the refrigerator and removed a long brown tube of something. "I lived in an apartment when I was in Minneapolis," he said. He took the tube to a cutting board and, taking a knife from a drawer, began to cut slices from it.

"When I came back to this area a few years ago I decided a house was what I wanted this time. I didn't necessarily need something this big, but when I saw this place I was sold. The realtor was practically dancing for joy, at the size of her commission I'm sure, when she saw she had me hooked. I couldn't hide it. This was the place for me and she knew it."

"I don't blame you. What's the view like in the summer?"

He smiled and said, "Even better. Here, try some of this." He held a round slice of meat out to her. "It's venison summer sausage."

She set her mug down next to his and took the piece of meat. She bit into it. "It's good," she said after a moment, and ate the rest of it. Suddenly ravenous, she took the second piece he offered and shoved it into her mouth. "*Mmmm.*"

"I knew you'd like deer meat if you gave it a chance," he said.

Jaws stopping in mid-chew, Riley stared at him. "*What?*" she said around the food in her mouth. Her eyes widened as the full horror of what he'd said dawned on her.

"Riley, I told you what it was," he said, seeing her distress.

She leaned over the sink and spit the last remnants of the meat from her mouth.

"No you didn't!" Her voice was muffled, her head almost in the sink. Turning on the cold water tap, she filled her cupped hand and drank.

"I *told* you it was venison summer sausage," he said, stepping closer.

Riley came up, and took the clean dishtowel he offered. She wiped her lips, then held the bunched-up towel to her mouth with both hands, her eyes on his. Her shoulders were shaking.

Aaron said, "I'm sorry. When I said venison I thought you knew that's deer meat. Everyone around here knows that—but I forget you're not from around here."

She was laughing as she lowered the towel and allowed mirth to take over.

"I didn't know," she said, gasping for air. "I was eating Bambi, and—and loving it."

Aaron relaxed. "I thought I was going to end up as the next batch of summer sausage around here," he said, a slow grin spreading across his face.

She shook her head, and wiped at the tears in her eyes with the dishtowel. "Please... next time you decide to feed me a member of the Disney forest, make sure it's absolutely clear to me what I'm eating."

"No surprise Thumper stew?" he asked.

She buried her face in the towel. "Oh, no!"

"I promise." He reached out, took the dishtowel and gently

wiped her cheeks with it. Their eyes met in silent commun-ication, as something between them continued to grow, cautiously, but with their mutual consent.

Reluctantly, Riley's eyes broke away and went to the clock on the wall, and she was surprised at how late it was. "I should get home. If Gran wakes up and finds me gone, she'll—"

"Ground you for a week?" he teased.

"Or take away my telephone privileges."

He gently zipped her parka up to her chin. "Then I'd better get you home before curfew, Red."

The ride back was companionable, filled with conversation about the upcoming Winter Games and the town in general, and when Aaron pulled up in her grandmother's driveway Riley was almost sorry to get out of the SUV. But it was late, so she thanked him and hurried up the steps to the front door. She opened the outer storm door, then turned and waved at him, keys in hand, and watched as the SUV backed out of the driveway.

She moved to insert the house key in the heavy front door, and as she did so the door swung slowly inward on its hinges.

It hadn't been closed all the way.

A tight fist took hold of Riley's heart and squeezed as a wave of cold fear ran through her. She looked quickly back over her shoulder for Aaron, but he was already maneuvering the SUV onto the road. He looked up and saw her, lifted a gloved hand in a wave, and drove off.

Reaching into her pocket, Riley retrieved her cell phone and kept it in hand as she stepped into the entryway, ready to dial 911 at a moment's notice even as she tried to convince herself it wouldn't be necessary. She was overreacting. She might not have pulled the door all the way shut when she'd left. But she was sure she had. She remembered the loud click the latch had made as the door closed, and she'd worried at the time that the sound would wake her grandmother. No, she was quite certain she'd closed the door all the way.

Farther into the house she saw that lights were on. Riley went in that direction, past the kitchen, to the sewing room. Her grandmother was there, in nightgown and robe, standing at her sewing machine, which looked as though it had been gutted.

Riley put the cell phone back in her pocket. "Gran, what's going on?" she asked, taking in the screws and pieces of metal scattered over the surface of the Singer's cabinet. The front cover of the machine was off, and the belt had been removed.

Looking up at her, obviously agitated, Bette said, "I wanted to sew, but I can't get this darned thing to work right. Someone's been messing around with my sewing machine again."

Riley stepped closer to look at the disarray. The sewing machine had been intact just hours earlier. "What do you mean messing around with it?" she asked. "Did you go outside? The front door was open."

"Someone came into the house and broke it. They took it all apart. I was trying to fix it, but I think parts are missing."

Riley slipped out of her parka, and draped it over a chair. She put a calming hand on her grandmother's arm. "Gran, who would come into the house?"

Her face twisted into a scowl, Bette angrily threw the hand off. "I knew you wouldn't believe me," she spat. "That's why I tried to fix it myself, before you got home. Where *were* you tonight? Where did you *go*?"

Though she'd seen her grandmother angry before—at the college boys who'd rented a cabin for a week and left it with broken furniture and gouged woodwork; at the contractor who took too long to finish the repairs to her front porch, then did a lousy job; even at a grocery clerk who'd put her carton of eggs on the bottom of the grocery sack and a container of orange juice on top of them—her grandmother had never been angry with *her*. The experience was so foreign that Riley didn't know how to react.

"I—I went out for a little bit," she stammered. "I left a note on the kitchen table."

But Bette wasn't listening. She'd already turned back to the sewing machine, her frustration growing as she tried to push the cover back into place despite the hanging belt and loose pieces scattered about.

"Here, let me help," Riley said. She reached out to pick up

some of the stray pieces, but Bette pushed her away.

"No, I'll do it. Did you take this apart? Did you do this?"

"Gran! Of course I didn't." Riley wanted to cry. She didn't know what she could do to make the situation better, or even what was really wrong. She wondered if her grandmother'd had a mild stroke, if that could be causing this frightening behavior.

"Who did, then?" Bette demanded. "People have been coming into my house. I hear them at night on the back porch. I see them looking in the windows."

Riley took a deep breath and moved between her grandmother and the sewing machine. "Gran, listen to me," she said, speaking in a low, calm voice. She put both hands on the older woman's shoulders, gently but firmly. "I'll help you to bed. In the morning we'll straighten this out together. Everything will be all right, I promise."

For a moment it looked as though she would protest, but then Bette seemed to shrink within herself and she nodded. Riley let out a sigh of relief.

Walking with an arm around her shoulders, Riley guided her grandmother from the room, to her bedroom. There she helped her out of her robe and into bed. She tucked her in, much the same way she herself had been tucked in when she was a child, visiting here in this very house.

"Turn the back porch light on," Bette said wearily, her eyes drooping. "That way they won't come back."

"I'll do better than that," Riley said, smoothing the blankets over her shoulders. "I'll leave the hall light on, and if you need anything at all you call out for me and I'll come right downstairs."

"Okay," Bette said in a soft, childlike voice. She sighed deeply, and turned her head. Within moments, she'd drifted off to sleep.

Standing there, Riley wondered now if her grandmother had been sleepwalking all along. It would almost make sense—she'd gone from being disturbed and angry, to meek submission, then to apparent sleep in such a short time. After a few minutes, when she was sure her grandmother really was down for the night, Riley tiptoed from the room, leaving the bedroom door halfway open. Out in the hallway she turned on the light as she'd promised.

As she stood there, she wondered if she would get any sleep herself.

SEVEN

"I could come three afternoons a week," the voice on the phone said.

Riley, sitting at the kitchen table with the phone propped to her ear, jotted down notes as the woman talked. Lauren had called earlier and given her the names and phone numbers of several women who might be able to lend a hand with some light housekeeping, and possibly even with the cabins.

"What about in the summer?" Riley asked her. "When the resort's going I think she'll need more help keeping the cabins in order between guests. Would you be able to expand your hours then if necessary?"

"You bet, shouldn't be a problem," the woman said.

Riley thanked her, and told her she'd get back to her. On the table in front of her was a yellow legal pad with some scrawled notes, phone numbers, and doodlings she'd made as she'd interviewed prospective help.

"Judy sounds promising," she said to her grandmother, who was at her computer a few feet away. "I didn't ask for references, but since Lauren gave me these names I'm sure they're all good."

Bette was sharp and alert this morning. Riley clung to this with renewed hope, more convinced than ever that the night before had been an aberration. Perhaps it really had been an episode of sleepwalking, as she'd considered the night before, but certainly nothing as serious as a stroke. They hadn't talked about the incident, and early this morning Riley had quietly slipped into the sewing room and put the Singer back together as best she could, hoping she'd found all the pieces.

Bette's fingers clattered on the keyboard as she typed. "My friend Glenna, in Ohio, just got married again," she said, turning from her computer to share this latest bit of e-mailed news with Riley. "She lost her husband a few years ago. Imagine that—she's my age and getting married. I'm happy for her. No one should be alone all the time."

Riley looked up from her papers. "What about you? Any hot prospects?"

Bette laughed, and dismissed the question with a wave of her hand.

"Aren't there any single men your age around town?" Riley persisted.

"Your Grandpa Joe spoiled me. I'd forever be comparing any new man to him." Bette tapped a key on the keyboard, sending her message to her friend in Ohio. "Now you, young lady—you don't have that excuse. Why are you still single?"

"Now you sound like Mom," Riley said. "I just haven't found the right one, I guess."

"If you're looking for perfection, you'll never find it," Bette said. "Even your Grandpa Joe had his flaws, few though they were."

"Right now I'm just very concentrated on my work," Riley said. "I'm in a competitive business, and I have to keep on my toes at all times to make sure someone else in the company doesn't pass me by on their way up. There'll be time later to think about dating."

"Don't wait too long. You're not getting any younger."

"Thanks, Gran, that's just what I needed to hear." Riley's tone was teasing, but her grandmother's words had struck a chord. Though she tried to convince herself that she did not need a man in her life, that career and the satisfaction of being self-sufficient were enough for her, there were times when she felt an indefinable sense of something missing. Like the canary in the cage, she was starting to look with longing at the open door in front of her.

Last night it had taken her a long time to get to sleep, but when she finally had she'd dreamt of Aaron's warm kisses on a cold balcony, and a cocoon of strong, protective arms around her. After waking, and remembering the incident with her grandmother, she'd longed to curl up and pull the covers over her head, to relive those few moments when she'd been taken away from herself, when all her troubles had seemed to fall away in the encompassing sensations of heat and longing, surrender and anticipation.

"Aaron."

Riley blinked and looked up at her grandmother, who was standing beside the table, the cordless phone in her hand.

"It's Aaron," Bette repeated, holding the phone out to her, an infuriatingly shrewd expression on her face.

Riley hadn't heard it ring, hadn't even been aware of her grandmother getting up from her computer to come to the table and pick up the phone. Riley took the phone.

The night before, on their drive back from his place, Aaron had promised to get her the names of a couple of handymen in the area who could do repair work on the cabins. He had those names for her now, as well as phone numbers. Riley wrote down this new information as he gave it to her, determinedly keeping her gaze from her grandmother, aware that her cheeks were flaming.

"Either one of them should be able to help you out with whatever needs to be done," Aaron said. "I've used them both myself, they're good men."

"Thanks," she murmured.

"Will you and Bette be at the Winter Games today?" he asked. His voice had an undertone of familiarity, giving a sense of intimacy to the simple question.

"Yes, we'll be there." Riley and her grandmother had talked about it, and they'd decided they would go to the event after lunch.

"Good. I'll be looking for you."

Bette was back at her computer. "You're certainly getting a lot accomplished in a short time," she said after Riley had hung up the phone. "I'm getting forgetful, and I seem to lose everything lately in a mountain of paperwork."

Setting aside her notes, Riley cleared her throat. This comment from her grandmother gave her the opening she needed. Casually, not wanting the question to sound as though it carried too much weight, she asked, "When's the last time you saw a doctor?"

"It's been a couple of years. My doctor retired and I haven't gotten around to finding someone new. Besides, I don't believe in going to the doctor unless there's something wrong."

"But you said you're forgetful lately. That might be a symptom of something." She hastened to add, "It could be something as simple as anemia. Maybe you just need vitamins, or an iron supplement."

"Do you think that could be it?" Bette's expression was heartbreakingly hopeful.

"We should find out for sure. If nothing else, you're overdue for a checkup."

"I don't know who I'd see."

"Let me take care of that."

With the help of the phone book, and a quick call to Lauren, Riley soon had the name of a female doctor, one who'd opened her practice in town within the past year.

"I think I'd like to see a lady doctor," Bette said when Riley filled her in.

Another phone call, she was placed on hold, and then Riley had an appointment for her grandmother for Friday after lunch, the soonest they could get in without it being an emergency. But that was still better than she'd hoped for, one of the advantages of being in a small town.

With that done, Riley stood and stretched.

Bette tapped away at her computer, bringing up sites for the family-tree research she was doing. "Did you know you have a great-great aunt by marriage who was a Heiltsuk Indian from British Columbia?" she asked.

"No, I didn't know that," Riley said. She went to the kitchen window and pulled the curtain aside. It was a beautiful morning, and she felt the need for some exercise.

"I belong to a genealogy club that meets informally a couple of times a month. We take turns at each others' houses. It's almost like detective work. I've been digging up old birth and marriage certificates online, finding relatives I didn't know we had. No one famous yet."

"Sounds interesting," Riley said. She turned away from the window. "I'm going for a walk. Want to come with?"

Bette's eyes were on the computer monitor, where images rapidly scrolled by as she manipulated the mouse in her right hand. "No, I don't think so," she said absently.

Riley hesitated, uncomfortable with the notion of leaving her alone in the house. "Are you sure? It looks nice out."

"I'm on a roll here. I want to stick with it."

Riley put on her parka and headed outside. She wouldn't be gone long, she promised herself, and she wouldn't go far. She didn't dare, not after what had happened the night before. But in the light of day it was difficult to imagine anything being seriously wrong.

She'd gone only a few yards along the trail behind the houses when Kirby, the neighbors' little terrier, joined her.

"Hey, fella, do they know you're on the loose?" she asked, scratching the dog's ears. His tail wagged appreciatively, and he fell into step beside her as though they'd been walking companions for years.

Her boots tramped down snow that was growing slushy from a recent warming, but it felt good to lengthen her stride and feel the pull on her leg muscles. Getting into the rhythm of it, Riley let her arms swing at her sides.

They'd barely rounded the first bend in the trail when a voice called out her name. She looked up to see Clay Johansen walking toward them on the path. This time, instead of his snowmobile suit, he was wearing the brown slacks and jacket of a DNR uniform, the legs of his pants tucked into heavy boots.

"How's it going?" he asked when he reached them. "Who's your friend?"

"He belongs to my grandmother's neighbors."

Clay bent and scratched Kirby's ears and around his neck, turning his collar. "He doesn't have tags. I wonder if he's licensed. It's the law around here."

"You aren't going to turn him in, are you?" she asked in alarm.

He frowned, then looked up at Riley and altered his expression to a smile. "Nah," he said, straightening. "But you might want to mention it to your neighbors if you see them. If their dog gets picked up and he's not licensed, they'll get fined."

Riley pulled Kirby protectively toward her. "Are you out collecting samples again?"

"Not today. I've been watching for trespassers. A lot of people around here post 'No Hunting' signs on their property, but the signs aren't always respected."

"Do you hunt?" she asked, thinking of the venison she'd eaten the night before.

"I have, but not lately. I've gotten more interested in conservation the past few years, in making sure there's enough land for the animals that live around here. We're squeezing them out as it is. I don't want to make it worse by hunting them."

She looked back over her shoulder. The roof of her grandmother's house was still in sight through the trees. "I'd better head back," she said.

"Everything okay?"

"Oh, sure. But I told Gran I wouldn't be gone long." He walked along beside her. To make conversation, she said, "We went to the mall yesterday, to a craft show, with Lauren Ross and her kids. Lauren and I used to be friends years ago, when we were kids. It's been fun running into her again, and talking about old times."

"I was a few years ahead of Lauren in school," he said. "Her family's been around here forever, like mine has. She was on a committee a couple of years ago that was trying to get our amusement park rebuilt and expanded into one of those big theme parks. Fortunately, that was voted down."

"You didn't like the idea?"

He shrugged. "I'm old-fashioned. The bigger it all gets, the more it becomes like any other city, without the charm that most of us here appreciate and don't want to lose."

They were near the house, and Riley slowed her pace. "There should be room for progress."

"I'm not against progress, as long as it's done sensibly and doesn't explode out of control, devouring everything in its path. That's one area where Aaron Wolfe and I don't see eye to eye." The animosity in his tone was harsh in the peaceful surroundings.

"I think Aaron values the area as much as you do," she

said, remembering the admiration in Aaron's expression when he'd shown her the view from his balcony.

But he shook his head. "Aaron Wolfe is just like the Eurasian water milfoil that's threatening this lake. He showed up here quietly a couple of years ago to run his restaurant, and since then he's been buying up property, grabbing whatever he can, taking it over a little bit at a time without most people even noticing what's happening."

"He's a businessman," Riley said.

Clay scowled. "He's a weed, slowly choking the life out of this town."

There were several yellow Post-Its stuck to the edges of her laptop screen, Riley's reminders to herself to attend to her work. She reluctantly logged on and checked her sites. There was no improvement, and another site, one for a preschool that was due to be launched soon and had been fine last week, was now also in the problematic category. She checked her inbox. There were two new messages from Joel. She read them, then fired back her own message asking about the problem with the preschool site. When she was done, she called her sister.

"I think I'm going crazy," she said as soon as Meghan was on the line.

"So what else is new?"

Riley got up and paced the small room. She heard a noise outside, and went to the window to pull aside the curtain. Below she could see the overhang of the front porch, and out on the walkway Clay Johansen was going by. She watched him for a moment to see if he was coming to the house, but he kept going and she let the curtain drop back in place.

"I picked probably the worst possible time to take time off from work," she told Meghan. "And the way things are going with Gran, I'm not sure I can get to everything that needs to be done here in the next couple of days."

"Why, what's going on with her?"

Riley gave her sister a rundown of their grandmother's episode of the night before, of her sometimes generally disoriented demeanor. She also told Meghan of her plans to get Bette to a doctor.

"I don't like the sound of this," Meghan said.

"It's even worse being here to see it. I can line up help for her—a handyman to work on the cabins, a housekeeper for around the house and with the cabins in the summer—but right now I'm more worried about her health. If we find out there's something seriously wrong on Friday . . . Meggie, how can I leave her?"

"But you said it might be something simple, like a vitamin deficiency."

"I can *hope* that's all it is, but we won't really know till she sees the doctor."

Bette called from the bottom of the stairs. "You almost ready to go?"

"Coming!" Riley called. To Meghan she added, "We're going to some winter festival thing. I guess it's a pretty big deal around here. Have you heard anything from Mom?"

"She called last night. The ship was docked at the Turks and Caicos Islands, and she's having a great time. She met somebody, an investment banker or something like that. She's all excited about it."

"Well, that's nice, I guess, if it's what she wants. I better go."

"Hey, keep me in touch with what's going on, okay? I feel bad that you're having to deal with this all yourself."

"That's not your fault," Riley said. "It's no one's fault. It's just . . . I don't know, but I'm glad I'm here with her."

The Winter Games was indeed a community-wide affair, and as Riley and Bette walked toward the amusement park from where they'd parked almost three blocks away, the crowd grew thicker, noisier, more boisterous. Kids ran everywhere, burning up energy, shouting with the pure joy of being outside on a weekday, the local schools having closed for the afternoon. Like the craft fair of the day before, the Winter Games was an opportunity for people to spend time together away from work and school, to have a little fun, socialize and just plain hang out. All of this was helped by the fact that it was a beautiful afternoon.

Riley kept her parka unzipped as she walked alongside her grandmother, taking in the sights, the food booths, even the bleachers and platform where a Winter Games king and queen would be crowned at the lighting of the bonfire later.

"How long has it been since you've had cheese curds?" Bette asked, heading toward one of the many food wagons.

"I don't think I've *ever* had cheese curds," Riley said, getting in line beside her grandmother.

"Then you're missing one of life's great pleasures. Your Grandpa Joe bought me cheese curds at the Iowa State Fair on our first date."

They moved up in line, and Riley looked at the pictures in the window of the wagon. Several people walked by, already sampling their cheese curds.

"Looks fattening," Riley commented.

"Very," Bette agreed happily.

They reached the front of the line, where Bette ordered curds for both of them, paid, and handed Riley a small paper bowl brimming with steaming yellow chunks of deep-fat-fried cheese. Riley looked at it uncertainly.

"My, that looks good," a voice said.

They turned and found that Geneva Myron was in line behind them.

Geneva gave them a friendly smile. "So nice to see you out, Bette. And your granddaughter is pretty enough to be crowned festival queen."

"Thank you," Bette said. "I agree, but she's not a resident so she's not eligible."

"That's too bad. Well, have fun, you two." She stepped up to the window and placed her order.

Riley and Bette found a bench to sit on.

"She doesn't seem so bad," Riley said.

"I suppose she was just being sociable," Bette added.

They looked at each other. "*Naaah*," they said together, and laughed.

Following her grandmother's lead, Riley picked up a small curd with her fingers and gingerly put it in her mouth. It was hot and gooey, very salty, and tasted sinfully wonderful, like every high-calorie food she'd avoided for the past ten years, all rolled into one sticky glob.

"This is pretty good," she said, surprised. She popped another curd, a bigger one this time, into her mouth.

"I thought you'd like them," Bette said.

"So Grandpa wooed you with these things?"

"He did. He also took me on the Ferris wheel, and he bribed the ride operator to stop it and keep us up at the very top for as long as he could—until the other people on the ride started to complain."

Riley looked at her grandmother and saw, beneath the weathered face, the young woman who'd once been there, and who showed through still in the sparkle of her eyes. "Did he kiss you while you were up there?" she asked. She put another curd into her mouth.

"You betcha. And a year later he took me on the Ferris wheel again and proposed."

"A whole year? Why did he wait so long?"

"He wanted to wait for me to turn eighteen."

"Eighteen! Gran, you were just a kid."

"Back then we tended to marry early, not like you girls these days. He was so handsome, and he was in college, so I was doubly impressed."

Her bowl of curds was half depleted, but Riley had slowed down in her consumption. They were very rich, and after a few they'd begun to lose some of their appeal.

Bette said, "Here comes Lauren, and it looks like she has a date. Good for her."

Riley looked up from her bowl. Lauren was walking toward them through the crowd. Wearing jeans tucked into knee-high boots and a short jacket, with her hair styled and wearing a touch of makeup, Lauren looked like a different person. Her arm was tucked through that of the man walking beside her. Balding, with wire-rimmed glasses, Riley recognized him as the man who'd been talking to Lauren at Aaron's bar the other night.

Lauren and her companion reached the bench. She introduced him to Riley and Bette, then he went off to buy some cheese curds and Lauren sat beside them on the bench.

"Stanley's the new dentist in town," she said, leaning in

close to them, her eyes bright. "I took Chloe to him a couple of weeks ago for her pre-braces exam. This is my first date in like three years. I was so nervous I changed clothes four times before he got to the house. I wanted to do something different with my hair, highlights or something, but there wasn't time. Do I look okay?"

"You look great," Riley told her.

Stanley returned and handed Lauren her cheese curds. When they strolled off together a few minutes later, Lauren looked back over her shoulder and waggled her fingers at Riley and Bette. Riley gave her the thumbs-up in return.

"Isn't that nice?" Bette said. "Lauren has found someone to share her life with, and she'll get free dental care for her kids."

"It's their first date, Gran. Don't start picking out a china pattern yet."

"I'm just saying it shows there are plenty of nice men around."

"I told you, I'm not looking."

Bette's eyes were scanning the crowd. "Oh, look, there's Clay. Clay, over here," she called out, raising her arm high.

Clay was headed purposefully toward them, and a suspicion began to form in Riley's mind. "Gran, you didn't tell him to meet us here, did you?" she hissed.

"No, no, nothing like that," Bette said innocently. "Though I might have mentioned it would be nice if we ran into him..."

Clay stood in front of them. "Hi. I wasn't sure if you said—"

Bette cut him off with a fluttering wave of her hands. "How nice to see you, Clay! Isn't this a great crowd for the festival? The best turnout ever, I think."

His expression cleared to safe neutrality. "Definitely a good crowd," he agreed. "The weather helps."

Their bench was getting crowded. A young couple with twins in a double stroller squeezed in beside Riley. She moved over for them, but this put her almost on her grandmother's lap.

"Some of my friends from the genealogy group are here," Bette said. She waved at several people, and an elderly gentleman broke from the group and came to the bench. Bette introduced him to Riley as Clarence Fitzpatrick.

He held out his hand. "Call me Fitz."

Riley shook the hand, but Fitz had eyes only for Bette. After a few minutes of small talk Fitz and Bette decided to join their friends to watch an ice-sculpture demonstration being done with a chainsaw.

"I'm just going to say hello," Bette said to Riley.

"You go ahead, I'll be fine," Riley assured her.

"Don't get lost, you two," Bette called over her shoulder as she and Fitz walked away.

Riley looked down at the remaining cheese curds in her possession. There were still several left but she felt stuffed, and she wondered what this impulsive snack was going to do to her complexion, her waistline, not to mention her self-respect. There was surely nothing of nutritional value in what she'd just consumed. "I can't finish these," she mumbled.

Taking the container from her, Clay threw it unceremoniously into a nearby garbage can. "Want to walk around?" he asked.

"Um, sure," she said, looking over at her grandmother, who was watching the ice-sculpture demonstration with her friends. "But not far."

"We'll stay in sight," he said. They walked a few yards to the edge of the frozen lake, where an impromptu game of broom-hockey was in progress.

"She put you up to this, didn't she?" Riley asked.

"Up to what?"

She nudged him with her elbow. "Don't play innocent. I know my grandmother. If there's a single man and a single woman within a hundred feet of each other, she'll try to get them together."

Clay smiled. "She didn't have to twist my arm."

She was comfortable with Clay, and didn't mind spending time with him here at the festival, but she hoped her grandmother hadn't offered him undue encouragement. The chemistry between them was so bland as to be almost nonexistent. He seemed nice enough, but no sparks flew when he was around.

"Are you going to be around for the bonfire later?" he asked.

"That'll depend on Gran. If she gets tired and wants to go home, we'll go."

"You could always come back," he suggested. "Or I could pick you up at your place, if you want."

Uh-oh.

"My place? Oh . . . you mean my grandmother's house. My place is in Dallas."

His pleasant expression faltered. "Right. I forgot. You seem to fit right in here, I have to keep reminding myself you'll be leaving soon."

"Not so soon. A few more days."

"Too soon for me."

She glanced sharply at him, but Clay had his eyes on the broom-hockey players. Riley watched the players also, and wondered at this sense of loss she was beginning to feel at the thought of leaving. It was ridiculous. This was not her home.

Some of the hockey players, two teenage boys and a young woman who looked in her early twenties, slid close to the edge of the ice, pushing and shoving for control of the small black puck. They were laughing, obviously having a great time. The woman's cheeks were rosy, and she gave it her all as she pushed one of the boys aside and swiped her broom at the puck, sending it shooting off in another direction.

Riley laughed at their antics, as did the people around them. Several more players got into the game, which seemed not to have much in the way of rules, so there were now over a dozen people of all ages and gender careening around on the ice. No one wore ice skates, they slid along instead on boots or heavy shoes. Balance was sometimes uncertain, and more than one player hit the ice and slid on a butt or stomach, only to get up and right back into the game again.

Just as she was about to suggest they walk back in the direction of her grandmother, a strong arm went around Riley's waist and pulled her away from Clay. She almost stumbled, but was held upright against a chest as broad and firm as a tree trunk, a tree trunk with a scent that was becoming familiar to her. Riley looked up into the face of Aaron Wolfe.

"C'mon," he said, steering her away from Clay. "You

haven't lived till you've experienced a game of broom-hockey."

"Aaron, I'm not sure . . ." she began, but he wasn't listening.

"Hey!" Clay protested. "She doesn't want to go with you."

Clay grabbed her arm, and for a moment Riley was in the middle of a ridiculous tug-of-war, about to be wrenched apart like a turkey wishbone at Thanksgiving. Aaron kept pulling her toward the frozen lake, and Clay was doing everything he could to prevent that from happening. About five seconds of that was all Riley could tolerate—she planted her boots firmly in the snow, locked her knees, and pulled her elbows in close to her body.

"Stop it!" she cried.

They both released her, and Riley glared from one man to the other. "What I'm *going* to do," she said firmly, "is go back to my grandmother."

"I just checked on her, she's fine," Aaron said. But he made no move to grab her again.

"Let's go, Riley," Clay said, his tone lofty. "I'll take you back to your grandmother."

She looked at him, his pleasant face and pale good looks. Then she looked at Aaron—dangerous, strong, his presence nearly overwhelming. Clay was non-threatening and easy to talk to. Aaron chafed, but he was always fascinating, whether he was grabbing her to take her out onto the ice, or to the second-floor balcony of his house for a few moments of intense, white-hot kisses.

Definitely, sparks.

Feeling overheated in the parka and heavy sweater, Riley had the desire to shed some clothing, to pull away the cumbersome sweater and give her skin room to breathe. She sure hadn't felt this way when it had been just her and Clay.

"I think . . . I think I'd like to give broom-hockey a try," she said.

This was crazy. She'd kill herself on that ice. But she stepped away from Clay's bland security into the maw of danger, where she might end up being ripped apart, but at least she'd have fun while it was happening.

Glaring at Aaron, Clay said, "Be careful, Riley. That's all I have to say."

As he walked away Riley watched him go, regret making her second-guess her decision. He'd done nothing to deserve being ditched. For a brief moment she considered going after him and apologizing for her rudeness. Then a strong, warm arm slipped around her waist again, and she forgot all about Clay Johansen.

"What's with you two," she asked, looking up at Aaron.

"Clay and I don't get along."

"Well, duh. But why? He seems okay."

Aaron tilted back his head to peer down at her. "We don't agree about a lot of things, but it kind of came to a head about six months ago when I was all set to buy the old train depot on the edge of town. Clay managed to get the sale blocked. He had it declared a historical fixture, or something like that. Now it just sits there and it's deteriorating, but by God no one's going to touch it."

A voice shouted nearby, and the puck slid along the edge of the ice with a mixed group of players in hot pursuit.

"Ready to give it a go?" Aaron asked.

Riley watched the players skeptically. "How do I keep from falling?" she asked.

"Like this," he said, and took both of her hands in his. He walked backwards out onto the ice, leading the way. "Relax, and don't overbalance. Give yourself time to get your footing. You'll get used to it. And don't go too fast."

"No trouble there," she said, feeling the smooth ice beneath her boots. Her heart thudded in her chest, but a sudden exhilaration made her laugh out loud.

Aaron took a broomstick from a pile on the ice and handed it to her. "Sweep like you're sweeping a floor. Aim for the puck but don't hit it too hard. It slides easy."

She held the broom handle in one hand, her other still in Aaron's. Then, slowly, he released her and she was on her own. She gripped the broom tightly, legs wide apart, wobbling precariously as she sought her center of gravity. Aaron got a broom for himself and came back to her, sliding expertly on his boots.

The puck flew past Riley's feet and she and Aaron were

suddenly surrounded by skidding, yelling, laughing people of all ages. Riley was bumped and she almost fell, but she managed to right herself at the last moment. Aaron was now too far away to help her. Several people had come between them, and all he could do was look over their heads at her and yell instructions.

"Get the puck!" he hollered, waving his broom.

She looked around. A man who had to be close to her grandmother's age elbowed Riley as he tottered behind his broom, pushing the puck forward. A group of pre-teens were trying to get the puck from him. The man turned, waving his broom at the kids, momentarily abandoning the puck, and Riley suddenly had an opening. She swung her broom at the puck, hitting it with all her might. It shot across the ice like a missile. Aaron was right—it slid easy. An astonished group of kids and one old man took chase after it.

Riley whooped and danced in place, holding her broom high over her head. "I got it!"

"Wrong way!" Aaron shouted, laughing.

He came gliding toward her, slid a little when he tried to stop and grabbed her for support, his arms going around her. For a moment it seemed they would both go over onto the ice, but at the last moment he kept them upright.

"What do you mean, wrong way?" Riley said when she'd caught her breath. "You said hit it, I hit it."

"Over there," he said, pointing, one arm still around her. "That's where our goal is."

She saw nothing but a big pile of snow flanked by a couple of scraggly-looking trees. "How was I supposed to know that? You never told me."

"You're right, I didn't. Sorry." Aaron continued to hold her close as he looked down at her.

"Get it!"

The puck flew past them again, followed closely by a young couple who shoved each other mercilessly as they each sought to gain control of the little black disk.

"There it goes!" Riley cried, and pulled away from Aaron. She turned and headed after the couple, skidding hazardously across the ice but determined to get the puck back and redeem herself.

She wobbled unglamorously, but managed to work her way in the direction of the other players, picking up speed as she went and using her broom as ballast.

"You're going too fast!" Aaron called from somewhere behind her.

Careening wildly toward the edge of the ice, toward the snowbank and the trees, Riley was no longer in control of where she was going. Someone bumped her, then someone else. It was all she could do to stay upright, and she knew she was about to go face-first into one of the trees that was coming up much too quickly. She couldn't think, all she could do was close her eyes, throw her arms up in front of her face and hope she wouldn't be too horribly disfigured by the impact—

Something hit her hard from the side and she was thrown violently off course, directly into the snowbank next to the trees. The impact turned her so she hit the snow with her shoulder and tumbled, cushioned by the soft padding of white fluff, but with something heavy on top of her.

Riley came up laughing and sputtering. The heavy thing on top of her was Aaron. He'd seen her heading for the trees, had caught up and tackled her, throwing her into the snow and preventing her from sustaining serious injury. She was on her back, looking up into the smiling face of the man she'd been thinking of so often lately, who invaded her dreams and infuriated her at times, and she felt not the cold of the snow she was lying in, but a molten inferno that grew and spread deep inside her.

"Get a room!" someone yelled with good humor, and there was accompanying laughter.

Looking down at her, Aaron brushed the snow from her hair and her cheeks.

He was smiling, but his eyes were deadly serious as he whispered, "Come to me tonight, Red."

EIGHT

Neither Riley nor her grandmother had much of an appetite for supper, but Riley made a salad with a light dressing anyway. They were both stuffed full of cheese curds, hot cocoa, bratwurst and sauerkraut, funnel cake and spiced cider. A salad would at least put something green and nutritious into their systems to counteract the junk they'd consumed at the park.

"You should've stayed for the bonfire," Bette said, spearing a cucumber slice with her fork. "Just because I was tired doesn't mean you had to come home, too."

"I didn't feel up to it anyway," Riley admitted. "I'm not used to all that fresh air and activity. Right now I'd kill for a nap."

Bette laughed softly. "I'll settle for an early bedtime." She carried her half-eaten salad to the sink and scraped it into the garbage disposal.

Watching her, Riley felt some of her worry dissipate. Her grandmother, though tired now, had shown no signs of confusion all day. Getting up from the table, she said, "I'm going to check on my e-mail upstairs."

Back in her bedroom, Riley brought up her work and found everything to be the same. She fired off another quick, frustrated message to Joel, then went to her bed and lay on it, staring up at the ceiling. The work was slipping out of her control, she could feel it, and that was something she'd promised herself she would not let happen during this trip. Vowing that tomorrow morning she would spend at least a couple of hours at the computer, Riley closed her eyes. She needed to rest, just for a minute.

A deep heaviness overtook her limbs, and she sighed. Just for a minute . . .

When Riley opened her eyes, the window in her bedroom revealed a black sky outside. She rolled over and looked at the clock on her dresser. Groaning, she sat up, and stretched her arms high over her head. She'd slept for over an hour. The nap had felt wonderful, but it would now be almost impossible for her to sleep again anytime soon.

Pushing up from the bed, she ran her hands through her hair. Her body protested, the ache along her calves and in her shoulders reminding her of all she'd done at the park earlier. She extended her arms high over her head and did a few slow stretches. It helped.

She thought of Aaron, and smiled at the memory of their tumble in the snow. He'd asked her to come to him tonight, and they'd both known what he meant. He wasn't talking about a few kisses on his balcony this time. At the time Riley had laughed, pretending to take it for a joke, but he hadn't bought it.

"I'll be waiting for you," he'd said before pulling her up from the snowbank.

But she'd already decided she would not leave the house tonight. Aaron Wolfe would have to understand. She was not going to take up with a man just because he had a killer smile and a way of making her feel, when he had his arms around her, like the world disappeared and nothing else mattered except getting more of that. Especially not when she'd be leaving in a few days, and would very likely never see him again.

But maybe, she thought, just maybe it was her impending departure that made the idea of seeing Aaron Wolfe again so attractive. She could allow herself the luxury of a brief, satisfying fling, enjoy it for what it was and leave it at that. Her feelings for Aaron were undeniably strong, but they were physical, a need brought on by the self-imposed isolation she'd been living with for too long. He was strong, sexy and available—a combination that she was finding irresistible.

But, no. She would not see Aaron tonight, and perhaps not again before she left. There was too much else going on for her to indulge a physical need, no matter how compelling.

Riley paced about the small room, restless, ready to jump out of her skin. The nap had worked wonders, and now that she'd stretched some of the stiffness from her muscles she felt invigorated, and full of restless energy.

She went downstairs to the kitchen, and was surprised to find her grandmother at the table, looking through her fabric samples.

"I thought you'd be in bed by now," she said.

Setting aside a bright, floral-patterned square, Bette yawned. "I'm going," she said. "I started looking at these fabrics and got caught up in plans for the cabins. But I've had enough for one day." She got up from the table, her bones creaking softly as she moved. She walked to Riley and kissed her on the cheek. "Thank you for taking me today, sweetheart. I had such a good time."

"I did, too," Riley told her. She walked her grandmother to her bedroom. "Gran," she said carefully, "I had a nap . . . and I was thinking I might go out for a little while after all. Would that be okay with you?"

She probably wouldn't go anywhere. She'd only brought it up because, on the off chance she did decide to, she wanted to make sure her grandmother knew about it.

But, most likely, she would stay in.

"You definitely should go out," Bette said at the bedroom door. "You're too young to be staying home all the time, just because I'm an old lady who wears out quickly."

"I might not," Riley hastened to add. "But in case I do, I wanted to let you know."

"Well, I appreciate that. Will you go back for the remainder of the bonfire?"

"Maybe."

"Lauren and her dentist will probably be there. You could find them."

"I wouldn't want to butt in on their first date."

"Clay Johansen will still be there, I'll bet. He'd be glad to see you."

"You're probably right about that."

Bette's expression turned sly. "Aaron Wolfe might even still be there."

Riley scowled at her grandmother. "Stop playing matchmaker."

Smiling, then yawning again, Bette went into her room.

Riley went upstairs and took a shower—just to wash off the day, not because she had anything special planned. The shower felt wonderful, and it further energized her. Afterwards she sat on the edge of the bed in her robe. She rubbed her still-damp hair vigorously with a towel, then picked up her hairdryer, leaned forward and let the blast of hot air fluff her hair.

This didn't mean she was going anywhere, it was just that she couldn't go to bed with wet hair. As her hair dried, the thick strands curled, and she used her fingers to ease out much of the natural springiness.

Maybe she *would* go back to the bonfire. She could find Lauren and—what has his name?—Stanley. She wouldn't impose, she'd just hang out with them for a while.

When her hair was almost dry, Riley ran a brush through it until it glowed like fire. Then she touched a little makeup to her face, and applied some mascara. She pulled on a pair of black jeans and a flattering black sweater she hadn't worn yet, and tiptoed downstairs.

She listened at her grandmother's doorway for a moment, and heard the steady sound of deep slumber.

Shoes in hand, she padded softly to the front door with a weird sense of déjà vu. This was too much like what she'd been up to in her mid teens, sneaking out at night to find trouble. She'd been an angry kid back then, more hurt inside by the divorce of her parents than she would have admitted, missing her father but also feeling betrayed.

But she was no longer that confused kid. She was an adult now, and knew what she was doing.

The bonfire was visible well before she reached the park. From her car Riley spotted revelers huddled around the blaze. She heard music, laughter, the sounds of many people, all having a good time together.

She drove slowly past. Her hands on the steering wheel and her foot on the gas pedal seemed to have taken on a life of their own, guiding her forward even as she chided herself that she was not going there.

But she knew she was.

She found her way to Aaron's house with no trouble at all. The porch light was on, as though in welcome.

Aaron opened the door while her hand was still poised to knock. With strong arms, he picked her up, kicked the door closed with his foot, and carried her into the living room.

He hadn't known if she would come. Surprised at the intensity of his desire to see her, he'd been incapable of playing it cool and letting her wait at the front door. Instead, he'd flung the door open and scooped her up in his arms, savoring the rush of feelings that shot through him too quickly for evaluation. There was the thrill of anticipation, certainly, but there was also annoyance with himself for letting the mere sight of her throw him into such a tailspin.

"I was hoping you wouldn't let me down, Red," he said, his face close to hers as he carried her to the big cushy sofa. A fire crackled merrily in the fireplace at the far end of the room.

He set her down on the sofa and pushed the red parka from her shoulders, letting it drop to the carpet. He kissed her, hard. Riley wrapped her arms around his neck and pulled him close, one hand on the back of his head, her fingers entwined in his hair.

His mouth was sweet and insistent, his tongue playful, then becoming more aggressive until he captured her mouth with his. Riley felt limp in a delicious, surrendering way that was unlike anything she'd ever experienced.

In the past she would have pushed him—or any man who exhibited such power over her—away, unwilling to surrender. She preferred to keep a tight rein on her emotions. But this passion that fired through her like a hot desert wind had her in its grip, and she surged forward to meet it head-on. If this was surrender, it was a willing submission, and she curled in to fit herself to him, marveling at the way their bodies moved together.

Somehow, without Riley being quite sure how it'd

happened, they were lying stretched out on the sofa.

It was too much, too soon. She had to pull away to catch her breath.

"What's wrong?" Aaron asked, his voice husky. His fingers, playing with the scooped collar of her sweater, brushed against her skin, leaving a trail of fire where he touched.

"Not wrong," she gasped. "Just fast."

He smiled. "Not fast enough, as far as I'm concerned." He leaned down and kissed the pulsing spot at the base of her neck. Poised above her, he kept most of his weight to one side, with one leg draped over hers.

"I wasn't going to come here tonight," Riley told him. "I tried to talk myself out of it. But . . ."

"You're here. That's what matters."

She sighed as his lips brushed against the hollow at the base of her throat, and traveled to her collarbone. He pulled the loose neck of the sweater aside to better access the tender flesh there.

Riley sat up, pushing him back with the palm of her hand. He went easily, but his eyes scanned her face for a sign of what she wanted. She didn't say anything at first, but just kept this distance between them as she inhaled deeply.

Aaron's expression was intense. Then he tilted his chin in the direction of the fireplace, where the snapping fire danced, sending golden shadows of light throughout the room.

"Since we missed the bonfire," he said, "I made one of our own right here. I don't have marshmallows, but I have some pretty good wine."

She said, "Wine is good."

Aaron stood. Beside the sofa there was a little table, upon which were a bottle of wine and two glasses. He filled each glass halfway with deep red liquid. Then, holding both glasses in his big left hand, he held the other out to her. Riley took it, and he pulled her gently to her feet.

After settling down carefully on the floor in front of the fireplace, Riley took the glass of wine he offered. She sipped it, wondering if she'd just gone from the frying pan into the fire, so to speak. On the sofa she'd felt overwhelmed by a surge of powerful emotions, of a longing that had swept through her and threatened to send her crashing into unbridled sensation. But being here, in front of a romantic fire that gave a warming glow to everything in the room, was no more conducive to clear thinking than being on the sofa had been. In an attempt to bring her tumbling center under control, she turned her attention to the wine.

"Kick your shoes off," Aaron suggested. "Get comfortable."

He sat beside her and, without waiting for her to comply, set down his glass and reached for her feet. He removed first one, then the other shoe and set them aside. His strong hands engulfed her stockinged left foot and he massaged it, his thumbs digging into the pad of flesh beneath her toes.

The effect was immediate. Riley was *so* glad she'd showered and put on clean socks, but that thought was quickly driven away by the delicious shiver that went through her at his firm touch. He kneaded her foot expertly, until every muscle of her body slipped into relaxation mode.

"*Mmmm*," she hummed deep in her throat. "That's feels wonderful."

"It's reflexology. I learned it in Taiwan. It's supposed to be relaxing." He massaged first one foot, then the other, until she was limp and compliant.

"Oh, it *is*," she murmured lazily. She set her wine glass aside, afraid she'd drop it as her muscles turned fluid. "When were you in Taiwan?"

"A few years ago. I was a consultant for a company that imported medical supplies, so I was going there pretty regularly for a while."

"Why did you stop?"

"I got tired of being away from home so much. Travel's fun for a while, but living out of a suitcase gets old. And my father was having some health problems about that time, so I wanted to be nearby in case he needed me."

"Did he?"

Aaron nodded. "He had some blockage in the arteries to his heart, and he had a triple-bypass. He came through it great, and when I was sure he was really going to be okay I did something I'd been wanting to do for a long time—I sailed from Boston, down along the east coast to my brother's place in Florida. I stayed and helped him run a karaoke bar down there for a summer."

"Geez—what *haven't* you done?"

He stopped massaging her feet, but sat with them resting comfortably on his lap. "Lots of things."

"Name one," Riley challenged.

"I've never before sat in front of this fireplace with a beautiful redhead."

"Good answer."

"Now, can I ask you something?"

"Shoot."

"Since you have a limited amount of time here—as you've pointed out several times—why did you waste so much of it driving up? Why not fly?"

"I don't like to fly," Riley said simply.

"I figured that much. But why?"

It's . . . it's not safe."

"It's a lot safer than driving. More people—"

"Oh, I know all that," she interrupted. "I know the statistics. But when I'm in my car *I'm* at the steering wheel. I set the course, and I'm responsible for getting myself from Point A to Point B. I'm not helplessly strapped into a winged missile, hoping the people up front are paying attention."

"You want to be in charge of your own destiny."

"Exactly."

"Fair enough. I tend to be the same way." He looked at her with an intensity that seemed to delve to her very soul. "You're obviously smart and accomplished, but you also keep a piece of yourself shut off from others, like someone who's been wounded and doesn't want to risk getting close to anyone."

"That's not true," Riley said. She was finding it difficult to breathe, but for a different reason now than earlier. She tried to pull her feet away, but he held onto them. "I'm close to my grandmother."

"I can see that."

"And I'm close to my sister, and her kids."

"I'm glad to hear it. What about your parents? You've told me they're divorced—where are they now?"

She managed to sit up, her feet still captured in his lap.

Reaching for her glass of wine, she sipped and welcomed the distraction as the liquid slid down her throat. She was tempted to ignore his question, or to change the subject. He was attempting to take her in a direction she didn't like to go if she could avoid it. She'd done enough self-analyzing in her twenties, that period of time when she'd confronted her demons and had, she'd hoped, put them to rest.

But not answering Aaron's question was not an option, she realized. Painful though it might be, she wanted to share this part of herself with him, even if it meant opening old wounds.

"My mother, as we speak, is on a cruise ship somewhere in the Bahamas," she said slowly. "I think she's decided she's been single long enough and she's on the hunt for a new husband. According to my sister, she's making some progress. My father died when I was in college."

"I'm sorry to hear that."

"I didn't see a lot of him after the divorce," she continued, her voice so small it barely rose above the crackling of the fire. "His job kept him busy. I asked him—when I was about fifteen, and my mom and I were butting heads—I asked him if I could live with him instead. He said no. He was gone too much with his work, and he wasn't really set up to have a teenager in the house."

Aaron reached out and, with his thumb, wiped a tear from beneath her eye. "And you've never asked anyone for anything since, have you?"

Riley was unable to answer. Her throat had closed up, the ache a painful constriction that choked her.

"What happened after he said you couldn't live with him?"

She forced the words past the knot in her throat. "I turned into the teenager from hell, to use my mother's exact words. I made some bad choices, but somehow I still managed to get into college. By my second year I was on academic probation and on the verge of flunking out. One morning I woke up with yet another hangover and some not very nice memories of the night before, and I finally opened my eyes to what it was doing to my life. And I knew I was sick of it."

With the help of a couple of pretty good counselors, she'd pulled herself up from that dark place. But the memory of it would always be there, along with the fear that it was still lurking just below the surface, ready to drag her back in if she let her guard down.

Slowly, his fingers gentle, Aaron slipped her socks from both feet. He massaged her bare toes, then the pads of her feet. "You're about to spill your wine," he said.

The glass Riley held in her hand was tipped dangerously, the liquid almost to the rim and ready to dribble onto her sweater.

"Oh!" She righted it, then brought the glass to her lips. It had been painful, this brief foray into her sordid past, but she felt better for it. As though the pressure of holding it all in had become too much to sustain, now some of that pressure had been released.

Aaron continued to press his thumb along the length of the inside of her foot. "This area here works to loosen the spine," he said. "Feeling better?"

"Much," she admitted. "Is the seduction back on?"

"What do you think?" He brought her foot up and kissed the tip of her pinky toe.

Riley sighed, and at the same time a thrill of excitement went through her. "I think you have a strange way of doing things, yet it seems to work for you."

He kissed the next toe. "Is it working for you?"

She set her wine glass aside again. "It's working for me."

"Good. Because, believe me, the last thing I wanted to do was spoil the mood." He set her feet aside and moved up toward her, the length of his body stretching out over hers, pushing her gently back until her head was resting on one of the convenient pillows. He leaned on an elbow, his left hand slipping under her sweater and resting on the flat of her belly.

Riley reached up and, with deft fingers, unbuttoned the top three buttons of his shirt. She'd been looking at that spot at the base of his throat, where a tantalizing peek of brown chest-hair showed, for two days, and she was determined finally to get a closer look. The result was satisfying—his chest was broad and muscular, as she'd known it would be, an inviting expanse that made her want to lay her cheek against it and listen to the beat of his heart. She settled for undoing another button. She was no idiot, she knew exactly where this was going—and for once she was ready to abandon those whispering doubts and enjoy what was to come.

He moved smoothly, pulling her black sweater up over her head and setting it aside, then, bending down to undo the top snap on her jeans, slid the zipper down about halfway. He lowered his head and put his lips to the smooth skin just below her belly button.

Riley inhaled sharply as his tongue traced a trail of fire along her skin, around her navel, then lower, to the lace edge of her panties.

"Oh, my!" she gasped a moment later. "Where did you learn *that*? No, never mind. I don't need to know. Just . . . don't . . . stop."

Propped up on one elbow, Aaron watched as Riley slept beside him. She breathed softly, her lips parted, one cheek pressed into the pillow.

How had *this* happened? Not the part about her being in his bed—that was great, and he wouldn't change anything about the experience—but how had Riley come to mean so much to him in such a short time? A couple of days ago he'd known nothing of her existence, yet somehow he now found himself deeply invested in her well-being, even though his original intention had been only for a few days of harmless fun.

A faint glow from his yard light outside came in through the window. It was enough for Aaron to watch her, to explore the planes of her face in these rare moments when she was unaware of his scrutiny. It was a luxurious experience, and he let his eyes drift over every feature, each faint freckle on the smooth skin, the tiny frown line between her brows that was there even in sleep, and that he loved because it was an indication of her personality. He'd always been attracted to strong women, and Riley was definitely that. Yet there was also, just beneath the surface, a conflicted vulnerability that made him want to wrap his arms around her and protect her from all harm.

Somewhere outside a night owl screeched, and Riley

stirred, rolling over onto her back. She opened her eyes slowly, stretching her arms over her head. When she saw him watching her, she smiled.

He moved in close and pulled her to him, so that her cheek was resting against his chest. She nestled in closer, one arm draped around his waist.

"*Mmmm*," she sighed. "This is so much more comfortable than the carpet downstairs."

He turned his head so his lips were in her hair.

"Oh, I don't know," he said. "I kind of enjoyed the carpet. And halfway up the stairs. And in this bed. All in all, I think we did a pretty good job of christening my house."

Yes, they had done a pretty good job of it. So eager that they'd been unable to keep their hands off each other, the hours of mutually satisfying exploration had left them exhausted until finally, in his bed, they'd collapsed into deep sleep.

Riley pulled back and looked around for her watch, which rested, with her neatly folded clothes, on a chair beside the bed.

"How did my clothes get up here?" she asked. Most of their clothes had been left in an untidy pile on the floor downstairs.

"I got up while you were sleeping and brought them up."

Reaching for her watch, she brought it close to her eyes and squinted at the hands. She sat up. "Oh, geez, I gotta go— it's almost morning!"

She swung her legs off the bed and grabbed her panties first, and pushed her feet into them. Aaron sat up and watched her dress. She put on her jeans, grabbed her bra and, after a moment's hesitation, set it aside and put her sweater on without it.

He ran a hand through his hair. "You don't have to go yet. It's still early."

"That's just it—it *is* early. It's 4:30 and I never should have stayed so long."

"She won't be up yet," Aaron said, knowing instinctively the source of her concern. He put one warm hand beneath her sweater and cupped a breast.

She turned and touched the palm of her hand on his cheek.

She said, "Gran's sleeping habits have been erratic lately. I just can't take any chances."

For a long moment he tilted his face into the curve of her hand, then nodded his understanding.

She finished dressing, but kept her bra in hand.

Wrapped in a blanket, Aaron went with her downstairs. He helped her with her parka—she stuffed her bra into the pocket—and walked her to the front door. She was disheveled and flushed, her hair wild, her cheeks nearly matching the auburn tint of her tangled curls. He thought she was wildly beautiful, a forest creature that longed to shed the ties of civilization but was afraid to do so.

"I'll be at the restaurant most of the day," he said. "Can you come over for a while? You haven't seen any of it other than the bar."

"If I can," she said, zipping her parka.

They stood in the open doorway as the cold air drifted around them, looking at each other. Aaron, wearing only the blanket wrapped loosely around his waist, was reluctant to let her go. He took the front of her parka with one hand and pulled her to him, lowering his face to meet hers. The kiss was long and deep, filled with remembered passion and the promise of more to come. He put everything he had into it—he wanted her to remember this, to take some of their night together with her like a blanket of her own.

He released her reluctantly. "Tell me I'll see you later," he persisted.

"I'll try," was the best she could offer, and she turned away.

He watched her walk to her car. Not until she'd driven away, after he'd climbed back in his bed and felt the emptiness of it without her did the doubts begin to reemerge.

This might have been a mistake. He had a full plate right now, he was busy juggling a dozen different business deals and an emotional involvement would be a distraction he couldn't afford. He was a lone wolf, so to speak, and it worked for him. Especially since the near-disaster of the financial setback he'd suffered before taking over the restaurant. That had almost broken him, and he intended to prove, to himself and others, that he could rebuild his finances to a state even better than before.

He would allow nothing to get in the way of his plans. Dalliances were fine—hell, they were a necessary part of life— but he had to remember to keep an emotional distance. If he could manage that, he'd be fine.

NINE

Bette stood at the stove, turning slabs of bacon with a fork. She hummed along to the radio as she worked, enjoying the sense of purpose that came with having another person in the house, someone to be aware of and to care for.

The loneliness of the past few years weighed heavily on her at times. It had prompted her to join the genealogy club after seeing a flier on the bulletin board at the public library, a step that had proven beneficial in that it put her in touch with people during these long winter months, when the resort was closed.

Drawn by the smell of the bacon, Riley stumbled into the sunlit kitchen. The table was set, and there was a cup filled with coffee waiting for her.

"I thought that would get you up," Bette said.

"I haven't slept this late in ages."

"It's all that extra exercise you've been getting. It's got you worn out."

Riley nearly choked on her coffee. "W-what?"

"At the festival. All that fresh air, and the broom-hockey. You're not used to the winters here. It'll take a lot out of you without your even realizing it."

"Oh . . . sure."

They sat at the table, and Riley attacked the food on her plate with gusto. "What do you want to do this morning, Gran?" she asked as she buttered her toast.

"A few members of my genealogy club are coming over in about an hour. You have a great-great aunt by marriage who was a Heiltsuk Indian—did you know that?"

Riley set down her butter knife. "I think you mentioned it."

"It's one of the interesting things I've learned about our family since I joined this club. Anyway, we were talking yesterday about some ancestor-trackings we've been working on, and we decided we're overdue for a meeting." She looked at Riley. "I didn't ruin any plans, did I? You didn't mention anything special yesterday, so I thought it would be all right to invite them over."

"No, it's okay. I didn't have anything specific in mind."

"You can hang around if you want, though I don't know how interesting it'll be for you."

"I'll probably go for a walk. Or I might go see Lauren."

"You should do that," Bette said. "You girls need to spend time together."

After breakfast, Riley went back upstairs. Aaron had extended an invitation she hadn't thought she'd have time to accept. Now she had time, and her mind went back to the night before, to the sweet kisses that had left her weak with yearning, to his hands on her skin, his palms that were rough from work, yet gentle as they'd stroked her.

A half an hour later, showered and dressed, she hurried down the stairs.

"Gran, I'm going out for awhile," she called as she took her parka from the hall closet. If she got to the restaurant early enough, Aaron would have time to show her around. She reached into the pocket of her parka.

Her grandmother appeared, wiping her hands on a dishtowel. "Take your time. My group tends to get long-winded. What's that hanging from your pocket?"

Riley pulled out what she thought was a glove, and found herself holding her bra.

"Oh, uh . . . " She shoved the bra back into the pocket, her face crimson.

"Better take that upstairs before you lose it," Bette said. She turned back to the kitchen, but not before Riley saw her lips twitching with a barely-suppressed smile.

Riley flew back up the stairs and threw her bra in the hamper in her bedroom, humiliated beyond words, praying her grandmother wouldn't see fit to bring this up again later.

"I'll be back after lunch, Gran," she called as she went out the front door.

There were only a few vehicles in the parking lot of the restaurant, and near the side entrance sat Aaron's SUV. Her heart raced at the sight of it. Not the SUV itself, but what it represented—Aaron was near, and she suddenly couldn't wait to see him.

She found him in the kitchen, talking to a woman who held a stack of menus. There were several people in the kitchen, all attending to their various jobs in preparation for the evening supper crowd, and they moved about as efficiently as worker bees in a hive. Aaron looked up when Riley approached, and the frown that had been creasing his brow disappeared as a smile transformed his face.

The woman with the menus barely glanced at Riley. "What are we going to do about this?" she asked, her voice strained. "We can't put them out this way."

"Just a minute, Virgie," Aaron said to her.

He went to Riley and gave her a brief but meaningful kiss on the lips, his hands on her shoulders. "I'm glad you came by. I didn't know if you would."

"I didn't know if I would either," she admitted. "But Gran already had plans with some friends, so she didn't need me around."

"Good news for me," he said.

"Aaron, people will notice this," the woman said. "We'll be a laughingstock."

Aaron's eyes stayed on Riley. "How did you sleep when you got home?"

"Like the dead. It took bacon and coffee to get me out of my room."

"Aaron . . ."

He turned to the woman. "I'll send the menus back to the printer, Virgie. It's their mistake, they'll have to fix it."

"That'll take days," Virgie said, holding out the offending menus as though they were contaminated. "What are we going to do in the meantime?"

"We can cross out the error and write the right word in on

each menu." He looked at Riley. "Sorry. But if you help, we can get it done even quicker. Then I'm all yours."

"Crossing it out will look terrible!" Virgie argued.

"What's wrong with the menus?" Riley asked.

"One word is spelled wrong."

"It's not just that a word is misspelled," Virgie huffed. Her cheeks had turned bright pink.

Throwing his head back, Aaron laughed.

"It's not funny."

"Yes, it is. Lighten up, Virgie. People will understand. Most of them will even see the humor in it."

"What's the word?" Riley asked.

Aaron looked at Virgie. "Go ahead, tell her."

Virgie struggled with what might have been a reluctant smile. "The cracked crab salad is described as... well, the word 'crab' isn't quite right."

"Our cracked crab salad is unfortunately described as 'cracked crap salad,'" Aaron finished for her.

Riley laughed, and this time even Virgie tentatively joined in. Opening one of the menus, Aaron pointed out the offending word.

"There may be a way to fix this so it will look better than just writing it in," Riley said. She asked Aaron a few questions about how the menu had been designed, and was glad to hear that he'd created the original on his office computer, which still contained the template.

In his office, Riley sat at the computer. She highlighted only the section on the menu they needed, and printed out multiple copies of it on plain white paper. Then she, Aaron and Virgie cut the sections to fit and inserted them in the menus under the clear plastic cover. It wasn't perfect, but it wasn't bad.

"This'll work," Virgie said happily. She left, menus in hand, to put them at the hostess table.

"Thanks. You saved Virgie's peace of mind," Aaron said, putting his arms around Riley's waist and pulling her close. They were still in his office, but the door was open and the busy kitchen was only a few feet away. "Now we have some time together."

Despite the people nearby, Riley let herself relax in his arms. The restaurant receded to a distant hum of activity as she rested her cheek against his chest, his shirt smelling crisp and freshly ironed, and closed her eyes.

A woman poked her head into the office. Her horn-rimmed glasses were perched on the end of her nose, and she peered over them. "Aaron, the electrician never showed up this morning to fix that light in the ladies' room, and Lee called in sick again so we're going to be shorthanded tonight. He's not sick. I happen to know he was at the Winter Games very late last night."

"Call Shaun to come in, he wants the hours."

"What about the electrician?"

"He'll get here. He told me if he didn't make it this morning, he'd come in the afternoon."

The woman left, and Riley said, "Busy place."

"Always. Come on, I'll give you the official tour."

He tried. Starting in the kitchen and going from there to the main room, every few steps they were interrupted by someone with a problem they wanted Aaron to solve immediately, or questions to be answered on the spot.

Men and women prepared the dining room, spread clean tablecloths over the tables, wrapped silverware, polished glasses. The busy sounds and the presence of others intruded.

"Come with me," Aaron said after a few minutes of this, taking Riley by the hand.

They crossed the room, and he pushed through a set of double doors. They entered the bar, which was quiet and shrouded in semi-darkness, the only light coming from a neon beer sign over the cash register. As soon as the door closed behind them, it was as though they'd stepped into another, more private world. The bar wouldn't open until much later in the day, and they were, for the moment, alone.

Aaron kissed her, his lips coming down on hers with an authority that recalled their previous evening together, and refreshed passion swept over them in the darkened room.

His hand was in her hair, his palm cupping the back of her head with a gentle pressure that held her to him. Riley lifted up on her toes and wrapped her arms around him, hunger filling her every cell.

From the other room came the sudden harsh sound of a glass breaking, a sharp intrusion that forced them apart, though the longing to touch remained. The double doors swung open, and a figure entered the bar. A young man in a stocking cap and fingerless gloves, carrying an open-topped box, entered.

"Oh, hi, Aaron," he said. He nodded at Riley. "That shipment of bar glasses you ordered has finally arrived. I'll—" He looked at them both, his expression changing. "I'll just leave them here on the bar," he finished, and set the box down.

"Thanks, Paul," Aaron said.

The other man left, and as the doors swung wide with his departure they saw Virgie, hands moving expressively, berating a young woman who stood with her arms crossed. Before the doors swung closed again Virgie looked up. She started to say, "Aaron—" when the doors closed on her words.

"I should get going," Riley said. It was obvious they would have no privacy.

"I'm not ready to let you go." He took her hand. "I have an idea."

Holding her hand, Aaron pulled her around behind the bar, past the cash register and through another heavy metal door—one she hadn't noticed before.

Cool darkness greeted them. Aaron flipped a switch and an overhead light came on. Around them were shelves holding boxes clearly marked with their contents—beer, wine, whipping cream, maraschino cherries.

"We're in the cooler!" Riley exclaimed.

He put his arms around her. "This might be the only place in the building where we'll get a minute to ourselves."

"If we don't freeze first."

"I'll keep you warm." He lowered his face to hers and kissed her again, his mouth very warm indeed, and insistent.

She burrowed into him, enjoying the embrace and his powerful presence. Despite the cold, she felt more alive now than she had in a long time, as though she'd been stumbling through the past few years of her life in a half-sleep without fully realizing it, and had only recently been revived to a state of awareness. His strength, at times overwhelming, lifted her to a realization of her own potential, and she suspected this sensation of hypersensitivity could easily become habit-forming.

They heard voices from the other side of the metal door.

"I'm sure I saw him in here a minute ago..." a muffled but still-distinguishable female voice said. Virgie.

Another voice, this one masculine, said, "Maybe he went out the back way."

"I don't think..."

Then yet another voice. "Where's Aaron? Someone said he was in here."

"Not here."

"Well, where is he? I need his okay to order a hundred and fifty pounds of sirloin . . ."

Riley put a hand up to her mouth to stifle a giggle.

"Okay, maybe this wasn't the best idea after all," Aaron whispered.

"What'll we do?" she asked, her voice equally low.

"We wait them out." He pulled her closer, and she buried her face in his soft flannel shirt. She'd left her parka in his office, and neither of them was dressed for an extended stay in a walk-in refrigerator.

A new voice joined those on the other side of the door. "Virgie, I need Aaron's signature . . ."

"He's not here. No one knows where he's disappeared to."

The sound of a chair scraping on the floor. "I'll wait. He's gotta show up sometime."

Riley grabbed a fistful of Aaron's shirt and pressed it to her mouth to smother her laughter. In doing so, she got some of his chest-hair.

"Ow!" he yelped.

"What was that?" one of the voices asked.

There was a moment of silence, then Virgie said, "C'mon, we don't have time to sit around here all day. There's a lunch crowd coming in."

"But . . ."

"Come *on.*" Insistent now.

The sound of the chair scraping again, then the voices

receded. Riley and Aaron waited a moment, holding their breath.

"I think they're gone," she whispered.

He opened the cooler door and peeked out. "Coast is clear," he said.

Riley's teeth were chattering. As they left the bar, went through the kitchen and to his office to get her parka, she imagined that everyone along the way was staring at them.

TEN

After leaving the restaurant, Riley went by the coffee shop. When she saw Lauren's car parked there, she pulled in.

"Hey," Lauren said, looking up from the register when Riley entered. "What're you up to today?"

If only you knew, Riley thought. Instead, she said, "Not much. Are you busy?"

"As a matter of fact, it's time for my break now that most of the lunch rush is over." Lauren called out to a plump woman who was wrapping silverware at an empty table, "Margo, would you watch the register for awhile?"

"Sure," the woman said.

Still chilled from her adventures in the walk-in refrigerator, Riley wanted only coffee. Lauren brought a sandwich and a bag of chips from the kitchen. They perched on swivel stools at the long counter that ran the length of the room.

"I've been offered the assistant manager position here," Lauren said. "It'll mean a raise."

"That's great," Riley said. Then she saw her friend's expression, and down-turned mouth. "Um . . . isn't it?"

Lauren poked listlessly at the sandwich on her plate. "I don't know. This is starting to feel like a career, and I'm not sure I want the coffee shop as a career. And besides that I just signed up for some night classes at the community college, and being assistant manager will screw that up because I'll be on call more, and I'll be expected to take care of all the problems that come up with the night shift. The night shift is staffed by teenagers—there are *always* problems."

"What classes did you sign up for?"

"A couple of business courses, to get me started. And later

I want to take classes on accounting and taxes for a small business."

"What is it you want to do?"

Lauren opened the bag of chips and set them on the counter between them. "You'll think it's silly."

"No, I won't."

"I want to open a real antique store. I've told you about the shop in my garage. Well, so far it's been more of a hobby than anything, but I'd like to build it into something more than that."

"Why would I think that's silly?" Riley asked. She took a chip and ate it.

Lauren was working at her sandwich, pulling off the crust and breaking it into small pieces. "Oh, I don't know. Antiques are big around here, and I love it, but it seems like everything's moving toward the Internet. I don't know if there's much of a future for the type of small business I want to do."

"There'll always be a need for face-to-face selling," Riley said. "The Internet can be a convenience in many ways, and a detriment in others."

"But even you work mostly on the computer. Everything's computerized nowadays."

"It can be very isolating, staring at a monitor all day," Riley told her. "Most of the interaction I have with people is through e-mail or on the phone, even when we're right there in the same building. You said the other night that it sounds lonely, and you were right. Last month one of my co-workers, a woman I've worked with for three years, had a baby shower. I didn't even know she was pregnant. I'd probably gotten an e-mail about it, but I was so wrapped up in my work that I forgot all about it. I ran out on my lunch break and bought a present."

"So you get caught up in your work. That's not a crime."

"It is if you forget there are other things in life," Riley said. She thought of Aaron, and their brief stay in the walk-in refrigerator. She smiled at the memory.

"What?" Lauren asked. Finished with her sandwich, she pushed the plate away.

Riley shook her head. "Nothing."

"So you don't think my business idea is crazy?"

"Of course not. I think it's a terrific idea."

"I wish I could be more like Aaron. I heard just this morning that he bought some rundown property out on Prescott Way—an old gas station, I think it was—and he's going to tear the building down to put up condos. He's never afraid to try something new."

"Hey, Lauren, I can't get this thing to work," Margo called out from behind the cash register. Some late-lunch customers waited while she punched at the keys on the credit card scanner.

"Guess I better get back to work," Lauren sighed. "Do you want to come over later to see my shop? It's probably not much by city standards, but I'm kind of proud of it."

"I'll see what my grandmother wants to do," Riley said. "But, yeah, I'd like to see it."

At the house a few minutes later, Riley parked in the driveway. She got out of her car and froze, keys still in hand. The door to one of the cabins was ajar, hanging open like a reproachful mouth.

"Gran?" she called, her heart in her throat, and headed in that direction.

She found her grandmother in Golden Oriole, the interior of which was a jumble of strewn pillows and overturned furniture.

Riley looked around at the devastation. "What happened here?" she asked.

Bette, a sofa cushion in her hands, glared at her. "I didn't do this!" she said sharply. "They've been at it again. They come in and destroy my things. They're trying to drive me off of my own property!"

"No, Gran—" Riley began.

"They want the land, they want to force me out because I'm an old woman, and take what your grandfather and I worked hard to build up."

Riley took the cushion from her grandmother's hands, too shaken to argue the point. "Let's clean this up," she said slowly, looking around, wondering where to begin.

"You don't believe me, do you?"

"It's not that. I just don't know why anyone would come in and do this. What would it accomplish?"

"I told you, they want the property. Your grandfather and I bought this land back when it was cheap. Do you know how much it's increased in value since then?"

"No, but I imagine it's a lot."

"It *is* a lot. And some people think it would be better if it belonged to them instead of me."

"*Who* would want to take it from you? Gran, give me a name—something I can work with," Riley begged.

But Bette wasn't listening to her. She was moving around inside the tiny cabin, muttering angrily, looking in closets, under cushions, as though searching for something.

"Please..." Riley said, feeling frightened and helpless.

She heard a car outside. Riley looked out the window and saw Aaron's SUV pull up in the driveway, and park behind her car.

He appeared at the open doorway a moment later, his eyes taking in the ruination.

Bette started again on her litany of accusations, railing against the unnamed people who were coming into the cabins, even into the house, trying to scare her off.

Aaron listened patiently, nodding as she spoke. He seemed to take it all in with complete seriousness.

"I see," he said when she told him she heard people moving around outside the house at night. "I can understand how that would worry you, being here alone most of the time."

Bette seemed to calm down with Aaron there, but Riley was confused. "What are you doing here?" she asked as soon as she had the chance.

"I came to see my two favorite ladies," he answered, giving Bette a charming smile. He put a hand on her arm, and she let him lead her from the cabin. "I'll take you back to the house. Riley and I will clean up out here later."

Bette went with him meekly, which Riley found amazing in itself. She stayed behind and tried to straighten up some of the disorder, fuming as she did so, her suspicions growing as she found a garbage bag under the sink and began to throw torn curtains and pillow stuffing into it.

Aaron returned to the cabin a few minutes later. "I think she's feeling better," he said. "She's lying down on the sofa, but I think she—"

"What are you doing here?" Riley cut in sharply.

He looked surprised, then said, "I told you, I came to see my two favorite ladies. What's wrong?"

"It just seems strange that you'd show up now, right when she's telling me that people are trying to take her property from her."

"What does one thing have to do with the other?"

She had to look away from him. What she was thinking was too much at odds with the way she'd felt in his arms recently. "I don't know. But she has a valid point when she says her land is valuable, and it is getting harder for her to take care of it, as you keep pointing out. So maybe there *are* people who'd like to get their hands on it."

"And you think I might be one of those people?"

Riley winced, ashamed of her own thoughts when her lips still felt bruised by his kisses. "No . . . I guess not."

"After you left the restaurant I made so many mistakes, got in the way so much, that Virgie finally told me to get the hell out of there for a while and let her run things."

Riley ran a hand through her hair.

"I can handle this," she muttered. "I came here to take care of things, and that's what I'm going to do." She squared her shoulders. "I'd better get inside. I don't want to leave her alone for long. She has an appointment with a doctor tomorrow, maybe we'll get some answers there. It's probably just a vitamin deficiency, or thyroid imbalance, something like that, something we can deal with."

He nodded and said, "I'm glad you're taking her to a doctor. If I know anything about your grandmother, she's probably long overdue for a checkup."

She carried the garbage bag from the cabin and made sure the door was securely locked. Aaron, beside her, didn't say anything for awhile, until his hand touched her shoulder, ran down her arm, and his fingers encircled her wrist. He pulled her gently around, forcing her to look at him.

"Riley," he said slowly, his eyes searching hers. "When you

take her to the doctor tomorrow, keep in mind . . . things might not turn out exactly as you're hoping."

ELEVEN

Hands poised over the keyboard, Bette sat at the computer in her kitchen. She stared at the screen, wondering why she couldn't remember how to get into her e-mail. She used e-mail regularly, yet now, puzzled by the intricacies of the machine, she was at a loss as to what to do next.

She'd tried to lie on the sofa for a bit, but had felt too restless to stay there. When her genealogy group had been here earlier she'd felt sharp and completely on top of things. They'd talked about various sites that were proving most useful for their searches, and she'd shared the progress she'd made on her own family tree.

It hadn't been until after they'd gone that she'd begun to feel confused, her mind going off in directions she knew were illogical even as she'd been unable to stop the progression of creeping irrationality.

Riley entered the kitchen looking worried, and Bette dropped her hands to her lap. She didn't want Riley to know about the trouble she was having. She felt foolish enough about the incident out in the cabin. At the time she'd really believed someone had been out there. But now, as she thought about it—hadn't she gone in there herself earlier? There'd been times lately when she would tear a room apart looking for some lost object, only to, upon seeing the chaos she'd created, feel her mind latching onto the idea that someone else must have done it.

It had to be age catching up with her. She felt normal most of the time, yet she recognized that it took her longer to process information than it used to. At times it was frightening, especially when she could feel an unfounded anger come over her, and she'd lash out at whoever was at hand. Last week in the grocery store she'd berated some poor young stock boy relentlessly. She'd actually accused him of *hiding* the crackers, because she knew exactly where the crackers had always been but they were no longer there. Not until he'd taken her two aisles over and shown her the rows and rows of crackers stacked there had she realized her mistake.

It was things like that, incidents that seemed to happen more and more lately, that had prompted her to call Riley in Texas and practically beg her to come. Riley would take care of things. She was a sensible girl, and having her here made Bette feel safer. Tomorrow she'd see the doctor, and would no doubt be prescribed some new wonder drug to go along with the pills she took for her blood pressure and for her cholesterol. The older you got, the more medications you took, that's all there was to it.

"I thought you were lying down," Riley said, her brow creased. "Is everything okay?"

"I'm fine," Bette said, forcing a smile. "I was going to look up a couple of things on the computer, but now I don't feel like it. I might do some sewing instead."

"That would be nice. Is it anything I can help you with? As long as I don't have to actually sew, that is."

"Did Aaron leave?"

Riley nodded. "He wanted to get back to the restaurant."

"He's so busy, yet he always finds time to stop here and ask if I need anything."

"Does he do that a lot?" Riley asked.

"A couple of times a month, more if the weather gets nasty. After Christmas we had an ice storm that knocked electricity out for a few hours on this side of the lake. Aaron came out here in that terrible weather to make sure I was all right. The house was getting cold by then, and he took me into town and made sure I was settled in at a friend's house—with heat—before he left me."

"That was nice of him."

"He worries that I have more here to take care of than I can manage."

Riley rubbed at her forehead with her fingertips. "He tells you that?"

"All the time," Bette said. She turned away from the computer to keep the blank screen from mocking her. "Maybe he's right. It's what everyone seems to be saying lately, so maybe they're all right and I'm wrong."

"You don't have to listen to everybody," Riley said. "You know what's best for you better than anyone else."

"I suppose." Bette sighed heavily.

"I was talking to Lauren a little while ago about the antique shop she has in her garage," Riley said. "I told her we might stop by later to see it. But I don't want to do that if you don't feel up to it. I have to tell you, Gran, you look all done in."

"I'd like to go to Lauren's. I get tired of being in the house all of the time."

They bargained for a bit, and finally agreed they'd go to Lauren's only if Bette managed to rest first.

Lauren opened the door to her garage, and flipped on the light. The inside of the building appeared at first glance chaotic, with chairs, tables and other wooden pieces stacked everywhere. The far wall was dominated by shelves that were filled to overflowing with the supplies of her trade—varnish and varnish remover, sandpaper, and brushes of every type and shape. There were unfinished restoration projects on one side of the room, works-in-progress everywhere, and neatly labeled crates against another wall.

"Wow," Riley said, following Lauren into the garage. "I had no idea you were so involved in this."

"She's obsessed," said Chloe, peeking over Riley's shoulder.

Jake had stayed in the house to watch TV, but Chloe trailed along as Riley and Bette explored the workroom and stepped carefully around the various projects.

"I think it's wonderful that you have this place," Bette said. She stopped to look at a piece of furniture with ornately carved legs and a slab of white marble on top.

"It's been a hobby for a few years, but I'm hoping to turn it into more than that someday," Lauren said. "That's an oak sideboard. As near as I can figure it was made in the late eighteen hundreds. I got it at an estate auction six months ago for . . . well, I got a good deal."

"She paid a hundred and fifty dollars for that thing," Chloe spoke up, obviously unimpressed by the piece.

"It was a bargain," Lauren said.

"I believe you," Bette said.

It was late afternoon, and after Bette had taken the promised nap, she and Riley had headed this way. The nap had done Bette good. She was clearly refreshed, the circles that had been beneath her eyes earlier all but vanished, and she had a new bounce to her step.

"Have you ever tried selling your antiques online?" Riley asked, examining a small wooden jewelry box. "Something like this would ship easily."

"I wouldn't know where to start," Lauren said.

"There are several good online auction sites you could use, but you'd pay a listing fee and then a percentage of your sales. I really think you'd be better off creating your own online store, and listing it with the major search engines to publicize it."

Lauren blinked. "God, it's like you just started talking a foreign language."

Riley smiled. "It's not as complicated as it sounds. I could help you get started, and show you a few steps that'll help you manage it. You'll need a digital camera. Do you have one?"

"The kids gave me one for Christmas."

"Then you're already halfway there."

"Do you really think I could do it?"

"I'm sure you can," Riley said, and smiled at her friend.

"You're sure you don't mind that I invited them?" Riley asked for at least the third time in the past hour.

"Of course not," Bette said, rinsing some utensils and setting them on the rack to dry. "As long as they don't mind whatever we can throw together for supper."

"They won't mind."

Riley had impulsively invited Lauren and her children over for supper. They'd been having so much fun that she'd temporarily forgotten that this was not her house to be inviting people to, and that her grandmother's fragile condition perhaps warranted caution in making rash plans. In a way, Riley was beginning to feel as though this was her home. That may have been in part because of the summers she'd spent here as a child, but she suspected that didn't account for all of it.

But Bette was undaunted by the prospect of impromptu supper guests, and her idea of throwing together whatever she could find put Riley's kitchen back home to shame. For a woman living alone, Bette Harrison had a surprisingly well-stocked pantry. She'd pulled out all the makings for a big batch of chili, and already the aroma coming from the simmering kettle on the stove was making Riley salivate.

She went to the pot, lifted the lid, and dipped a spoon into the thickly bubbling mixture.

"That's hot," Bette warned.

Riley lifted the spoon to her lips. "Yow!" she squealed, dropping the spoon in the sink. She poured herself a glass of water.

"I warned you."

By the time Lauren and her children arrived a short while later, they'd set the kitchen table, forsaking the formal dining room in favor of this more comfortable space, and the chili had cooled to only three-alarm status. Jake and Chloe sprinkled grated cheese on their chili, while Riley, who preferred soda crackers, crumbled several and dropped them into her bowl.

"We have chili at school almost every week," Jake said, taking a spoonful into his mouth.

"Jake . . ." Lauren said.

He reached for more cheese. "I'm just saying this is better. The school stuff is canned. They add onions and think we won't know, but the empty cans are right there in the trash."

"I'm glad you like it. I like having people to cook for," Bette said as she poured milk for Chloe.

"You have Riley here," Jake said.

"Yes, but that's just for the week. She'll be going home in a few days."

"She should stay," he said. Then, to Riley, "You should stay."

Riley wiped her mouth with a paper napkin. "Texas is my

home. And I have a job there to go back to."

"But you could move here if you wanted to."

"Why would anyone pick Iowa over Texas?" Chloe said to her brother. "I'd love to live in Texas. Anything would be better than this hick town."

"You can go to Texas any time, I won't stop you," Jake said, then ducked, laughing, when Chloe swung at him.

"Chloe, keep your hands to yourself," Lauren said. "And I felt the same way when I was your age. I wanted to get out of here, too."

"So why didn't you?"

"I did for a while. I moved to Boston right after high school and lived there for about a year."

Chloe's spoon stopped halfway to her mouth. "You did? Why did you come back?"

"I got homesick. I missed my family and my friends, and I realized that I preferred small town living to the big city."

"My grandfather, Riley's great-grandfather, was from Texas," Bette said. "When I visited him as a child he'd make chili with goat meat in it."

Jake, eyes big, looked at his nearly empty bowl. "Is there goat meat in this?"

"Idiot," Chloe sneered.

Bette smiled. "No, just plain ol' hamburger."

The phone rang. Riley who was sitting closest, got up from the table.

"What did you do in Boston, Mom?" Jake asked.

"I worked in my cousin's antique store. I liked that, but I missed home."

Riley picked up the phone. "Hello?"

"Come see me tonight."

Aaron's voice in her ear made Riley's knees go weak. She looked over at the kitchen table. The four people there were busy eating, talking, laughing; no one was paying attention to her. "I can't," she said softly into the receiver, turning her back to the others.

"You can slip out quietly later. I need to see you."

"I just can't. Besides, I know what you have in mind."

"Would that be such a terrible thing?"

"No," she admitted.

He sighed, the sound coming through low and mournful through the receiver. "As much as I'd like to get my hands on you again, that's not entirely what I had in mind. There were a few things left unsaid between us today, and I think we need to talk about it."

Riley winced. "You're probably right, but not tonight."

"I think about you all the time, Red. You've got me howling at the moon."

Riley couldn't help it, she laughed.

All conversation stopped, and everyone in the kitchen turned to look at her.

"Who is it?" Bette asked.

She had no choice but to tell the truth. "It's Aaron."

"Tell him to come over, there's plenty here for everyone."

"I don't think . . ."

"Aaron, come on over," Bette called. "We're having a chili feast."

"With goat meat!" Jake yelled, and milk squirted out of his nose when he burst into laughter.

". . . then Janice, my head chef, performed the Heimlich maneuver on the guy. If you've ever met Janice you know she's one powerfully built lady. She works out, and if she wanted to I think she could toss me across the room."

Riley laughed as Aaron told his story, as she'd been laughing since he'd arrived a few minutes earlier.

"Did she save the guy's life?" Chloe asked. She stared at Aaron with open admiration in her large brown eyes.

"She probably did," Aaron told her. "But Janice also cracked two of his ribs in the process, and the piece of meat that flew out of his mouth shot across the table and hit his wife in the face."

"Wow," Jake said. "I always wanted to Heimlich someone. We learned how in school, in health class."

"Which you got a D in," Chloe said.

"Chloe," Lauren said. "Be nice."

"What'd I say? It's the truth." She turned back to Aaron. "Was he grateful? Did he give her a reward?"

"No reward. In fact he's suing us for the cracked ribs."

"Really?" Riley asked.

"We'll probably end up settling. It's easier, and cheaper in the long run."

Most of the dishes had been cleared from the table, but they all stayed in the kitchen, surrounded by easy companionship and the lingering aromas of the meal.

Beneath the table something nudged Riley's foot, then moved up past her ankle to the curve of her calf. Sitting directly across from her, Aaron feigned innocence, but she knew it was his stockinged toe that was working its way up her leg.

The front doorbell chimed, and Bette got up from her chair. "More company."

Gasping when the toe tickled her skin, Riley yanked her leg away. Her knee whacked the underside of the table in the process and the table jigged violently, making the remaining glasses rattle and tilt.

Lauren grabbed her water glass before it could tip over. "Jake, stop fooling around."

"I didn't do anything."

Bette returned to the kitchen with Fitz Fitzpatrick in tow.

"I was passing by and saw all the cars," Fitz explained. Bette found an extra chair for him and he squeezed in between Chloe and Aaron. Chloe, who'd been leaning on one elbow as she stared at Aaron, sat up and frowned at the intrusion.

With her legs tucked in under her chair, Riley stayed out of reach of Aaron's teasing big toe. Her cheeks still burned at the brief touch of his foot traveling up her leg, and she was glad for the distraction of this latest arrival.

"Where were you headed, Fitz?" Lauren asked.

The lanky man shrugged out of his coat, which Bette took and hung on a hook by the kitchen door. "I'm meeting Clay Johansen over this way. He wants to show me an area of wetlands he says is eroding or something. He thinks some wildlife will be in danger because of it. I'm on the city council, you know, and Clay is petitioning to have the wetlands protected."

Bette offered Fitz a glass of red wine, which he accepted

and downed with gusto. Glasses were passed around and more wine was poured, bringing a sulk from Chloe who announced that in Italy children were routinely allowed to drink wine with their meals.

"You'll just have to move to Italy, then," Lauren said, but declined a glass for herself to avoid an ongoing argument about it with her daughter.

"Will Clay wonder where you're at?" Bette asked Fitz.

"Nah, I'm not supposed to meet him for 'nother hour. I was just driving around, looking at the lake. Thaw's gonna come early this year. That'll make for a good tourist season. How're your reservations so far?"

"I haven't done any advertising yet," Bette admitted. "I have a couple of regulars already booked for the July fourth week, but not much else."

"Aren't you listed in the directory?" Riley asked. This was routine. Her grandmother's resort, like most of the others in the state, advertised regularly in a directory that had its own website and was seen nationwide. Early reservations were important to a business that ran for only four months out of twelve, and by this time her grandmother should've had her summer already half scheduled.

"I may have missed the deadline to renew," Bette said vaguely. "I'm not sure. I'll take a look at it . . ."

"We can look at it tomorrow," Riley said. It was too late to do anything about it tonight, and she didn't want anything to cast a pall over this evening. With her fingers on the stem of her wineglass, her eyes scanned the group around the table. It was good to see the room filled with people, friends all, enjoying an evening of talk, a little wine and laughter.

She had a sense of belonging here, one she realized now she hadn't felt in awhile. Happy for the moment, and unwilling to let any worries interfere with these feelings, she looked across the table at Aaron. Listening to something Chloe was telling him about school, he gave the girl his full attention and she, in return, blossomed like an early spring flower.

Next to his mother, Jake was flopped loosely on his chair, his arms dangling at his sides and his face tilted to the ceiling as though he'd been shot through the heart. His position suggested boredom now that no one was paying attention to him, but Riley suspected his sharp little ears were taking in every word being said in the room.

Lauren was talking to Fitz and Bette about her antiques. Fitz asked her about some old LPs he had in his attic.

"Depending what they are, they might be collectibles—but take them out of your attic immediately," Lauren said, waving her finger at him. "It's hot and probably dry, and those old vinyls will get brittle if they stay up there."

Aaron reached for the wine bottle in the middle of the table. He freshened his glass, then held the bottle up with an inquiring lift of his eyebrows to Riley. She shook her head and put a hand over her glass, which was still half full.

Momentarily distracted by Jake, who'd begun to emit gurgling noises, Chloe paid them no mind.

Aaron came around the table and leaned down to speak softly near Riley's ear. "I'm going out onto the porch for some air. Join me?"

She nodded, pushed her chair back and stood. He helped her up, his hand warm and enveloping on her arm through her sweater. His fingers went easily all the way around, his touch light and intimate.

They were almost at the kitchen door when Chloe, jumping to her feet, said, "I'll go too. Can I?"

Riley smiled at the girl, hiding her disappointment.

"Sure," Aaron said.

"No," Lauren said at the same time.

Already halfway around the table, Chloe ignored her mother.

"Chloe, stay here," Lauren said firmly. She caught Riley's eye for a fraction of a second, but it was long enough to convey all that she understood.

"But I want to go out on the porch," Chloe protested. She looked at Riley and Aaron, determined to put herself between them any way she could.

"No, stay here," Lauren said.

"*Why?*"

"Because I'm going to help Bette with the dishes, and you can certainly pitch in."

"We'll be back in a minute," Aaron promised.

"But I need some fresh air, too," Chloe said stubbornly.

"You can have all the fresh air you want after the dishes," Lauren said.

Chloe sulked, she whined, all of which did her no good. Her mother would not let her out of helping with the dishes, and Riley and Aaron headed out to the front porch.

So much for slipping quietly outside, Riley thought.

They didn't bother with coats, and once out on the porch Aaron immediately took her in his arms. "Think we fooled anyone?" he asked, one hand pushing her hair aside so he could nuzzle her neck.

"Not for a minute. That little girl has a crush on you. Thank goodness Lauren . . ." Then she faltered, unable to finish as his lips moved along her skin, sending shivers down her spine and curling her toes in her shoes. Aaron's fingers moved aside the collar of her sweater. The fabric was an unwelcome barrier that Riley longed to shed. She felt as though she could run naked through the woods, bare feet burning deep prints in the snow, and she would feel nothing but this unrelenting heat that permeated her very fiber when she was with him.

But this was a hopeless situation. They couldn't stay out here forever. There were people nearby, people who would look at them when they returned, who had sharp eyes that would catch the flushed cheeks, the sharp edge of frustration. Even knowing this, Riley couldn't move away, was powerless to resist.

A board creaked.

They pulled apart, separating to allow a slightly more presentable appearance to their inflamed embrace. Riley tugged at the hem of her sweater, which had somehow crept up.

"Hello. Nice night," a masculine voice said.

Riley put a hand to her cheek, which was as hot and smooth as a freshly ironed shirt. Aaron stiffened as he shielded her, facing the figure that came slowly up the porch steps. The scent that came through his clothing was sharp and predatory.

"What are you doing here?" Aaron snarled.

Riley smoothed her hair back from her reddened face. From within the house came the sound of laughter, muted by the closed doors, but still filtering out onto the porch.

Clay Johansen stepped up onto the porch. He smiled despite Aaron's tone, which had been harsh and unwelcoming. "I'm supposed to meet Fitz," Clay explained. "I saw his car parked out front here, and I wanted to make sure he hadn't forgotten."

"He didn't forget," Riley said, stepping out from behind Aaron. "He mentioned to us that he's meeting you later. He's right inside—do you want to come in?"

"Thanks," Clay said.

Aaron moved slightly, just enough to block Clay's way to the door. Taller than Clay, Aaron glowered down at him, his eyes narrowing with a dangerous intensity, bristling with implied threat. He looked a breath away from tossing Clay off the porch.

"Fitz is expecting to meet you later," Aaron said. "I'm sure he won't forget."

Jaw set, Clay stood his ground. "I was invited in."

"Not a good idea."

"That's not your decision to make," Clay pointed out. He took another half-step forward, so that he and Aaron were almost chest-to-chest, each glaring fiercely with primal hostility.

"I'm telling you—"

Riley moved forward, wedging her arm between them and pushing until she was able to put herself physically between the two men.

"Aaron, I invited Clay in," she said, looking up at the man who, only moments before, she'd been so hot for she would have fallen into a snowbank with him if that's what he'd wanted. But Clay had a point.

Eyebrows drawing together in disapproval, Aaron glanced at her, then returned his attention to Clay. But he moved aside, conceding this small defeat while still letting his displeasure be known.

Riley opened the front door, and Clay followed her in.

"Look who's here!" she said in a bright, cheerful voice as

they entered the kitchen.

Fitz and Jake made room for Clay between them. Bette, when she learned Clay hadn't eaten yet, insisted on serving up another bowl of chili. Stubbornly, Aaron refused to sit. Instead he stood by the refrigerator, arms crossed at his chest; his expression might have been that of a petulant child if not for the menace radiating from him.

"Clay's worried about some of the wetlands around here," Fitz said, reiterating what he'd told them earlier. "He's going to show me some areas that are in danger."

"How can you see wetlands in the middle of winter?" Aaron asked.

"I know where they're at," Clay said mildly, tasting the chili. "He'll be able to see the new construction that's gone up in the past couple of years and what it's doing to the area."

"We studied about wetlands in school," Chloe said. She glanced at Aaron, who kept a steely watch on Clay. "If they disappear, the animals go someplace else to live."

"I'm sure it's a valid concern," Bette said.

"It is," Clay agreed. "I'm hoping to widen some of the watershed boundaries, because we have some threatened wildlife around here that will be in danger if we don't protect their habitat."

"What about the people around here?" Aaron said, his tone belligerent. "What about their habitat?"

"I'm not suggesting people should leave. I've lived here most of my life, and I wouldn't want to be displaced. But we need to be responsible, we need to protect our environment or there won't be anything left to protect in a few years."

Chloe shifted her attention from Aaron to Clay. "That's what my teacher says."

"You can protect important pieces of land without bringing progress to a complete halt," Aaron said, his eyes boring into Clay.

"I'm all for progress—"

"I don't think you are. I think you'd like to see this whole area turned into one big national park, with access limited to tree-huggers like yourself—"

Clay pushed back his chair. It scraped on the linoleum with

a loud grating sound that cut through the room.

Riley put up both hands. "Whoa, there," she said loudly.

Clay, who'd moved to get up from his chair, froze. Aaron, still at the sink with his arms crossed, kept his scowl in place but said nothing.

"You're both forgetting this is not some town hall meeting where you can hash out your differences," Riley said. "This is my grandmother's kitchen. No animosity is allowed here."

"What's a tree-hugger?" Jake asked.

Clay relaxed in his seat. "You're right," he said to Riley. "Sorry, Bette."

"Don't apologize," Bette said.

Clay picked up his bowl and took it to the sink. He thanked Bette for the chili, then reminded Fitz of their plans.

Getting his coat, Fitz said, "Bette, I'll give you a call tomorrow."

Riley walked them to the front door.

At the door Clay turned to her and leaned in close to speak softly. "I didn't see you out walking this morning. I watched for you."

"I've been sticking closer to the house," she said. "It seems whenever I leave Gran for too long, something happens."

"Is everything all right here?" His brow furrowed with concern.

Riley shrugged. "I'm sure everything will be fine."

"Call me if you need anything," he said. "Even if it's just to talk."

"Thank you," Riley said. He was being kind, and she appreciated it.

She closed the door and leaned her forehead against it for a moment, savoring the sensation of cool wood against her skin.

TWELVE

Doctor Bernadine Gilbert was in her fifties, with hair that was cropped almost as short as a man's, and kind eyes behind her rectangle glasses. She came out to the waiting room to introduce herself to Bette and Riley. She took Bette's hand briefly in both of hers as they chatted. Then, after asking Riley to wait, she took Bette back to an exam room.

Riley sat nervously in the waiting room, an open magazine on her lap. She flipped through the pages without seeing anything, fighting the urge to jump up and pace about the room.

Other patients nearby waited their turn. A little girl sat on the floor, coloring in a tattered coloring book with crayons that were well-used nubs, while her mother read a paperback. An elderly couple sat near the window, their heads close, talking in low voices.

Riley set the magazine aside. She couldn't just sit here. Clutching her cell phone, she went outside to the sidewalk, then speed-dialed her work number.

"Emily, it's Riley," she said when she had her boss on the line.

"Riley, hello," Emily said, her voice cool almost to the point of indifference. "How are things going in Indiana?"

"Iowa. And I'm not sure . . . but I might have a problem getting back to the office when planned."

There was a long pause, then Emily said, "You're having that much fun?"

Riley sat on a low brick ledge next to the front door of the medical clinic.

"My grandmother is having some health problems," she said. "She's with the doctor right now, but if she needs to get regulated on some new medication I won't be able to leave till she's doing better."

There was another silence on the other end. "How long are you thinking?" Emily asked.

"Maybe a few more days." Riley mentally crossed her fingers, hoping that's all it would be.

"You know there's been a problem with a couple of your accounts. The Carpet Gallery site is a mess right now. Pages all in the wrong order, and some of the links are missing. That site's supposed to be launched early next week. How is that going to happen if you aren't here to take care of matters?"

"I'll take a look as soon as I get back to my laptop—"

"Never mind," Emily cut in. "I'll turn that one over to someone else. But let me know when you have a better idea of when you'll be coming back." She hung up.

Riley closed the flip cover of her phone, then got up from the ledge and went back inside the building. The waiting room was just as she left it, but as she entered a young nurse in a pink lab coat approached.

"Are you Riley?" she asked, smiling yet somehow managing to look serious at the same time.

Riley nodded.

"You can come with me," she said. "Doctor Gilbert and Mrs. Harrison are waiting for you."

Riley followed on legs that seemed heavy and slow to respond to her brain's commands. "Is everything all right?" she asked.

The young nurse opened a door. "Right in here."

Riley entered the small room. It contained a desk, behind which was a wall holding several diplomas authenticating Dr. Gilbert's credentials. The doctor was sitting behind her desk, and Bette was in a chair facing her. There was an empty seat beside Bette, which Riley took. She reached over and took her grandmother's hand.

"Mrs. Harrison has given me permission to speak with you about her medical condition," the doctor began.

Cancer, oh God, I knew it, Riley thought, and felt her meager breakfast roil around in her stomach.

The room swam. Riley closed her eyes until the feeling of vertigo subsided. Then, forcing an outer calm she didn't feel, she looked at the doctor.

"I believe Mrs. Harrison may be in the early stages of Alzheimer's disease," the doctor told her. "We've gone through a few cognitive tests. Of course, none of this is conclusive, but I've seen enough of it over the past few years that I feel confident about the diagnosis."

The words hit Riley like a blow. The doctor and Bette both waited for her to say something, but Riley had nothing to offer. She felt frozen, frightened, too numbed by those terrible words to formulate an intelligent response.

Bette spoke up. "Dr. Gilbert says there are some medications that might help."

The doctor nodded. "Some of the recent studies are promising. I want to refer Mrs. Harrison to the Mayo Clinic in Rochester. It might be possible to get her into a clinical study for some of the new medications. There are a few that haven't yet been FDA approved, but have been shown to help slow the progressive memory loss. I believe there are even more advancements on the way, and if she could get into one of these clinical studies she'd be in the early group for whatever is yet to come."

Riley found her voice. "You mean as a guinea pig?"

"As a way to help us all understand this disease better, and find hope in treating it. But we're getting ahead of ourselves with that. First, she needs to see a neuropsychologist at Mayo for a definitive diagnosis. That will tell us a lot more about how far it's advanced."

"*If* that's what she actually has," Riley said, searching for some small ray of light to cling to. "You said you did a few cognitive tests. That sounds pretty vague to me. You could be wrong."

"I could be," the doctor conceded. "That's why I want Mrs. Harrison to see someone who specializes in neurological disorders as quickly as possible. My nurse is making some phone calls right now, to get your grandmother set up with the preliminary appointments."

Bette got to her feet. "I'll go see how she's doing with that," she said. After nodding to the doctor, she bent and tenderly kissed Riley's cheek. "It will be all right."

After the office door had closed, Riley turned to the doctor. "It isn't going to be all right, is it?"

Dr. Gilbert ran a hand through her short, salt-and-pepper hair. "That depends on a lot of things."

Riley lowered her face to her hands. As an attempt to shut out the world, the gesture failed miserably. Her thoughts still intruded. They battered her tired mind like a small ship against the rocks, until she felt as though she would break apart under the assault.

"You could be wrong," she repeated, looking up.

"It's possible, but I don't believe so," the doctor said. "Haven't you wondered yourself, Miss Harrison? You made this appointment for your grandmother for a reason—you were concerned about memory loss, and confusion. Didn't that put up some warning flags for you?"

Riley raised her head. There could be no more hiding from this. "I thought it would be something else. I was terrified that it might be cancer. I never thought . . ."

But hadn't she? She wondered now if she'd deliberately skittered around the more sinister possibility of dementia because for this there was no recovery, and no hope.

"There's always hope," the doctor said, as though reading her mind.

"For what? A cure?"

"No." The word had a sad finality to it. "There is no cure yet, and this disease is progressive. But there is the hope that one of the new medications will slow your grandmother's memory loss and help stabilize her moods. She could function quite well for a long time to come, it varies so much from person to person."

"But she's been working on our family tree on her computer. She's at it almost every day. Why hasn't she forgotten that?"

"The daily repetition probably helps keep it fresh in her mind. For now."

Riley wanted her grandmother here with her. She wanted to put her arms around her and tell her everything would be all right, just as her grandmother had done for her when she was a little girl.

A single hot tear slipped down Riley's cheek.

Aaron stood beside his SUV, which was parked across the street from the clinic. He watched as Riley walked with her grandmother to her car, then helped her get settled in the front seat. Once that was done, Riley walked toward him. He straightened as she approached.

"How is she?" he asked.

Riley stopped two feet in front of him. Melting snow dripped from the eaves of the buildings behind him, the steady *plink-plink* like gunshots to his hypersensitive nerve endings.

"The doctor thinks it's . . ." The words stopped in her throat.

Aaron reached out and pulled her to the sidewalk, out of the way of oncoming traffic. He put his palm on the side of her face. "Tell me."

She looked up at him. "She thinks it's Alzheimer's. Gran has an appointment at Mayo in a couple of weeks to be sure, and to go over treatment options, and . . . and . . ."

He pulled her to him. He wrapped his arms around her, feeling her bones beneath her sweater. She seemed fragile, as though she would break apart if he applied too much pressure, but he was unable to release her. He wanted to hold her close and absorb some of her pain, take it from her and into himself. He was strong, he could carry this burden for her.

"I'm sorry," he said, his head bent to hers.

Riley didn't resist his embrace. Aaron felt selfish for taking advantage of the situation, but he relished her nearness, not caring for the moment what had brought it on. Tragedy though it was, if it brought this woman into his arms even for a little while, he could not wish it away.

"I'll follow you home," he said.

The words seemed to break the thin thread of her surrender. Riley pulled back, though he tried, briefly, to keep her close.

"No, don't do that," she said.

Aaron wanted to roar with frustration. The tenuous connection was already dissolving. She was so determined, always, to handle things herself. "You don't need to be alone in this, Riley. Let me help."

"You can't. No one can help." Her eyes shimmered with bright tears.

"I'm going to work in my sewing room for awhile. Sewing always relaxes me," Bette said after they'd hung their coats in the closet. "Unless you want something to eat first?"

"I'm not hungry," Riley said. "Are you?"

"No." Looking drained, Bette went to her sewing room. Within a few minutes the machine was running. The steady *whirring* was a soothing sound that drifted out to the hallway, and to the kitchen where Riley stood, wondering what to do next. They'd talked about the doctor's findings on the drive home, but their conversation had been limited mostly to the upcoming appointment at the Mayo Clinic, and what the doctors there might prescribe. Neither of them had felt ready yet to explore the deeper implications of the diagnosis, though Riley knew that conversation would have to take place soon.

She went to her grandmother's computer and, after Googling Alzheimer's disease, brought up everything she could find on the subject. She'd always considered herself fairly well informed on a wide range of subjects, but the sites she found had so much information that Riley quickly realized how little she'd really known. She read until the words began to blur before her eyes, then she printed out a few relevant pages.

From the other room she heard the continued drone of the sewing machine.

In search of a pen, Riley opened a couple of drawers beside the computer. She came to one that was stuffed with papers, most of which seemed to be old bank statements. More signs of the careless bookkeeping that Riley had noticed lately. Some of the folded papers in the drawer were legal-sized, and these Riley removed and looked through. Many were old and irrelevant. Then she found two pages that looked like they'd been stapled together at one time. Riley scanned both pages, noting at the top that they were pages two and three of four. She sat down to read, and within the dense script she caught key phrases and land descriptions that, with slow dawning, brought the importance of these two pieces of paper to light.

What she held in her hands, she realized, was an offer to buy the Harrison Lakeside Cottages. Her grandmother's property, everything she owned in the world. But with the top page, and more, missing, Riley had no clue as to who the proposed buyer was, or even when the document was dated. Feeling newly anxious, her hands shook as she read through the script again, looking for something, anything, she might have overlooked.

The machine in the other room had fallen silent. Papers in hand, Riley went to the sewing room.

"Gran," she said as casually as she could, "I found these in a drawer. Have you had an offer on the resort?"

In the process of pinning a hem on a length of fabric, Bette looked at the papers in Riley's hand. She frowned. "I don't think it was an offer to buy," she said. "It was... I think it was something to do with rezoning the docks on this side of the lake. Or it might have been about the ice shacks. Some people want to regulate how big they can be."

Riley felt sure this had nothing to do with either zoning or the ice shacks. "Where's the rest of it? Did you sign anything?"

"I keep my important papers in the file cabinet next to the computer. It should all be in there."

"I found these in a drawer. It looks like a couple of pages are missing. Gran, did you sign anything?" she repeated, unable to keep the anxiety out of her voice.

"No. At least... I don't think so."

Riley smoothed the papers, thinking. It wouldn't do either of them any good if she upset her grandmother. "I should take a look at the whole document for you. Do you know where the rest of it is?"

"In the file cabinet next to the computer."

"No, these were in a drawer." Riley's grip tightened on the papers.

Her grandmother's eyes glistened with distress. "I don't think it's important," she said, her voice wavering. "It was just something for me to look over. We have council meetings every month. I go to every one of them, there's always some new issue being brought up."

Taking a deep breath, Riley said, "It's okay, Gran. I just

thought I should look through any papers you have, just in case. When did you get this?"

"It's been a couple of weeks, at least."

Riley's heart sank a little. If the papers were indeed part of a purchase agreement on the property, and if her grandmother had signed it, every day that had passed since would make it more difficult for the damage to be undone.

"Do you remember who gave this to you?" she asked, very gently.

"Oh . . . you've met him." Bette waved a hand that trembled slightly in the air. "It's just . . . it's just something he wanted me to look over. He said it wasn't all that important, but it would make things easier for me."

I'll bet he did, Riley thought.

The front doorbell chimed, and they sighed in unison, both relieved at the interruption. Riley knew she'd reached an impasse with her grandmother, and that she'd have to look for the rest of the document on her own.

It was Fitz at the door. He'd stopped by, he explained, to show Bette a new genealogy website he'd discovered.

"I found it this morning," he said as they led him into the kitchen. He sat at the computer with easy familiarity. "I couldn't wait to show you," he said to Bette as she pulled up a chair beside him.

"I'm going upstairs to work," Riley said. She folded the papers in her hand. She needed time to think. "Fitz, are you going to stick around for awhile?"

"This could take some time," he said. "There are several interesting features about this site I want to go over with your grandmother." He gave Bette an affectionate glance. "Is that a problem? Do you need the computer?"

"No, not at all," Riley assured him. "Take all the time you want."

Upstairs in her room she spread the partial document out on her desk.

You've met him, her grandmother had said. That could be almost anyone. So why, Riley wondered, did her thoughts turn to Aaron Wolfe? She felt disloyal, frightened, and deeply conflicted by the suspicions that kept surfacing in her mind where Aaron was concerned. When she was with him, when she could look into those intense eyes, she knew there were layers to the man she hadn't begun to touch on. Just how ambitious was he? Enough to buy the business out from under an old woman? Her instincts told her no, he wouldn't do that, and her heart insisted she could trust him, but her head, her stubborn, quarrelsome brain, cautioned her not to trust a man she'd known only for a few days.

She needed to talk to a lawyer.

Flipping through the phone book, she found several listed in town, but after calling a couple she soon realized she would not get in to see anyone until Monday at the earliest, and none were willing to give her advice over the telephone based only on the vague information she had to offer. Disappointed, she finally made an appointment with an attorney for Monday afternoon, and got that only by begging and stressing the importance of the situation.

The phone book also revealed several real estate companies, but Riley had no idea which, if any, might have been involved in the creation of the document. Rubbing her forehead, she tried to will away the headache that was forming behind her eyes.

The phone rang, making her jump. It was Lauren.

"I'm so excited about this," Lauren gushed almost before Riley could get a hello out. "I've been taking pictures with the digital camera like crazy. The kids are even getting into it. This is the first time I've seen Chloe enthusiastic about anything in ages."

"That's great," Riley said, forcing enthusiasm into her voice.

"Can you come over later and show me a few things? I've downloaded some pictures into my computer already, but I don't know how to crop or edit, or any of that stuff to make them good enough for a website. You said you can help with that—right?"

"Sure, I'll show you some editing basics. You'll get the hang of it in no time."

"Do you and Bette want to come over for supper later? Then you can show me a few things on the computer after."

"Uh, sure," Riley said absently, not really hearing Lauren. Her eyes were on the two pieces of paper again, searching for anything that would help her unravel this mystery. "Lauren, do you know any of the realtors in town?"

"Probably all of them. Why?"

Riley hesitated only for a moment, then she told Lauren everything—about her grandmother's appointment with the doctor, the terrible diagnosis that still had her feeling as though the world had been tilted crazily on its axis, and the ominous-looking pages she'd found and her grandmother's uncertainty as to precisely what they were or where they'd come from.

"Oh, God, Riley, this is awful," Lauren said. "Why did you let me go on about my stupid pictures? My favorite uncle had Alzheimer's. It was awful, but every case is different and that was four years ago, there are probably all kinds of new therapies now to help your grandmother."

Riley blinked back tears. "I need to find out where this document originated," she said. "I can't even tell if it came through a realtor, or a law office, or where."

"Call Ronnie George, he's in the phone book," Lauren said. "Ronnie has a real estate agency and he has his finger firmly on the pulse of this town and everything else within a hundred mile radius. If it's anything to do with real estate in the area, he'll know about it even if he's not directly involved."

"Gran thinks it's something to do with zoning, but she was pretty vague."

"Doesn't matter, Ronnie will know. Tell him you're a friend of mine. I've known Ronnie since high school, and he still has a bit of a crush on me."

"Thanks," Riley said. She hung up, then looked up Ronnie George's agency in the phone book. She called, but was told he was out of the office showing some property.

"Have him call me as soon as he comes in," Riley said, giving both her grandmother's number and her cell phone number, and invoking Lauren's name for good measure.

When Riley next looked at the clock she was shocked at how late it was. The sun coming through the bedroom window was considerably lower, the elongated shadows like reaching fingers. She was also newly aware of the fact that she'd not heard her grandmother's or Fitz's voices in quite awhile. Getting up from her desk, she went downstairs.

"Gran?"

The kitchen was empty. The computer was still on, the screensaver glowing, but otherwise it was abandoned. A check through the house told Riley that it was empty. Panic lodged in her chest, a growing balloon of dread that threatened to burst.

Back in the kitchen, she saw a note on the table she'd overlooked earlier.

> *Went for milk. Back in a few minutes.*
> *Love, Gran*

THIRTEEN

How long ago had her grandmother gone? It might have been only minutes, but somehow Riley doubted that. Though she'd been unaware of the house's silence on a conscious level while upstairs, now it seemed to her that it had been that way for quite awhile.

The stillness in the kitchen was a harsh rebuke, a reminder that she was frighteningly alone with this problem. The house itself spoke of sorrow and neglect in many small ways, and Riley felt the reprimand that came with it. She'd ignored the signs for too long because she'd been wrapped up in her own issues. Her websites no longer seemed important. They were important to others, she knew, to the clients who counted on the Internet to increase their business. But Riley couldn't reconcile that to what mattered most in her own life. Her grandmother mattered. Her mother and her sisters, her niece and nephew, those she held dear to her heart, even Lauren and Aaron—they were what she valued.

Without bothering to grab her coat, Riley went outside to the garage and stood there for a moment looking at the open door, the empty interior. She didn't feel the chill that came with the lateness of the day.

She ran back inside and grabbed the phone book, flipping to the yellow pages. There were only three grocery stores in town, and it didn't take long for her to call each one and establish that her grandmother had not been to any of them. She left a message at each one for her grandmother to call home if she showed up.

Then she looked up Fitz's number, and called him.

"Well, I left well over an hour ago," he said in response to her question. "Bette didn't say anything about going out. I would have offered to take her if she'd said she wanted to go someplace. We do our grocery shopping together sometimes."

Riley thanked him, and hung up.

Her options were narrowing. The only thing left to do was drive to town and look for her grandmother's car. She might have decided to stop at the post office for stamps, or one of the little shops. There were many possibilities, none of which need be ominous. Riley wrote her own brief message of her whereabouts on the back of her grandmother's note, and included her cell phone number. Just in case.

She got her parka from the hall closet, and went out to her car.

On Main Street Riley scanned the parking spaces in front of the shops for her grandmother's car. A few people waved as she went by, and she waved back. The town had regained some of its old familiarity, and even those people she hadn't met in the past few days seemed to know who she was. Under different circumstances she would have appreciated being made to feel so welcome in the small community, but at the moment all she could do was drive, and pray that she would soon find her grandmother.

She drove around for an hour, as the sun dipped lower in the sky. Main Street consisted of only a few blocks, but there were side streets that branched off and held an expanding business district. Other than those shops that catered strictly to the summer tourist trade, many of the businesses were still open year-round, and a few stayed open late on Fridays. There were beauty salons and clothing stores, a picture framing shop, several interior decorators, as well as dentists, lawyers and accountants.

She parked, and went into a quilt shop on a side street that she knew her grandmother frequented.

"Have you seen my grandmother, Bette Harrison?" she asked the woman behind the counter.

In her early sixties, petite and silver-haired, the clerk was thumbing through a sales catalog. She straightened, massaging the small of her back. "Not since last week," she said. "You're Riley, aren't you? She told me you were coming for a visit. Goodness, she talks about you a lot. All about your job, and your exciting life."

Not so exciting, Riley thought.

"If you see her, will you tell her I'm looking for her?" Riley wrote her cell number on a scrap of paper.

The woman took it with an expression of concern. "Is everything all right?"

"Oh, sure," Riley said, not wanting to cause alarm before she knew for sure there was something to be alarmed about. She managed a smile that didn't feel right and probably looked just as bad. "We've just crossed wires is all. Thanks."

She left the quilt shop and walked into the store next to it, a Hallmark card store. She left her phone number there as well, and also in the next one down the line, a thrift shop. She was leaving her phone number on bits of paper everywhere, like bread crumbs dropped on a trail deep in the woods, with the hope that the trail would eventually lead somewhere.

Back in her car she continued to drive, covering territory she'd already gone over, but not knowing what else to do. She turned the car's headlights on as the street lights glowed to life.

It was after six o'clock and she'd been searching for over two hours. The sense of dread grew more insistent, becoming a knot that sent shivers throughout her body. She gripped the steering wheel of her Mustang, wishing she knew the twisting side roads better. There were so many of them that wound through the woods around the lake, some so narrow that they barely accommodated two cars at a time. If her grandmother had driven onto one of those roads, for whatever reason, Riley feared she would never find her on her own.

At a loss as to what to do next, she turned onto a road she recognized, and pulled into Lauren's driveway.

"I don't like this one bit," Lauren said. "Maybe you should call the police."

Riley paced in Lauren's kitchen. "I hate to do that. What if she stopped at a friend's house? I'd be putting out an alarm that would worry everyone and embarrass Gran."

"Better to be embarrassed now than to do nothing and have to call for a search party at midnight."

"I'll check back at the house. She might be there,

wondering where *I'm* at right now."

"You said you left her a note with your cell number."

"She might not have seen it. She gets confused."

"More reason to call the police."

"Not yet," Riley said. "I want to look on my own, just a little longer."

Chloe came into the room, a mink stole draped over her arms. "This thing stinks like moth balls or something. Should I hang it on the line overnight to see if the smell comes out, or— oh, hi, Riley." Her eyes brightened. "I'm helping mom get things set up for our store. "

"That's great," Riley said. She forced herself to examine the stole Chloe held. "Airing it out might help. If not, you can go online and research ways to clean vintage clothing."

"Okay. Mom, can I go on the computer?"

"For a while," Lauren told her. To Riley, she added, "I know a lot of Bette's friends. I'll call around and ask if anyone's seen her."

Riley nodded, and said, "Call me right away if you hear anything. I'm going to check at the house again." She headed for the door.

"Keep me posted," Lauren said on the front porch.

When she pulled up in her grandmother's driveway, Riley saw that the garage door was still open and the interior empty, just as she'd left it. The house had a dark, forlorn sense of abandonment to it. She backed up again, out of the driveway. Then she stopped and rested her forehead on her hands, on the steering wheel.

It was full dark, and even the headlights of her car didn't completely cut through the deep gloom of the evening. The moon was partially obscured by clouds. The streetlights did little to help, and the tangled branches of the tall trees around the lake added a sense of menace.

She knew she could no longer do this alone. Driving around all night, on unfamiliar roads, she was likely to get lost herself. Lauren was as concerned as she, but other than making a few phone calls there was little else she could do. With her kids in the house, Lauren wasn't free to drive around to help look along the side roads Riley didn't know as well.

Lauren was right. She needed help with this, and for once Riley was going to ask for it before it was too late. Lifting her head, she put the car in gear and drove in the direction of Aaron's restaurant.

The parking lot of the restaurant was already three-quarters full with the Friday night supper crowd, but Riley found a space and ran into the building, her parka unzipped and hair flying behind her as she bypassed the startled hostess at the entrance. She found Aaron standing near the doorway to kitchen, clipboard in hand, talking to Virgie. Head tilted, Virgie nodded as she pointed at the clipboard with a pencil. They both looked up in surprise as Riley approached, flushed and breathless.

"What's wrong?" Aaron asked, handing the clipboard to Virgie.

Riley had enough presence of mind to keep her voice low, though she could see people watching them with open curiosity. "I can't find my grandmother anywhere," she said.

Aaron took her arm and they walked toward his office. With his head down almost to hers, he asked, "How long have you been looking?"

"A couple of hours. I've been driving around, hoping to spot her car somewhere." She told him about the note on the kitchen table, her visit to several downtown businesses, and her increasing fear of the worst. "Do you think she stopped at a friend's house and just forgot to call me?" she asked, almost begging him to confirm this hope.

"No." He reached inside his office door and retrieved his jacket from the hook there. "We'd better go look for her."

Weak with relief that she didn't have to do this alone any more, she nonetheless had to ask, "Can you leave your restaurant when it's busy like this?"

"Don't worry about that. I have a good staff, they'll keep an eye on things." He pushed his arms into his jacket, spoke a few words to Virgie, then came back to Riley. "Let's go," he said.

His SUV was parked at the side entrance of the building. Once inside, Aaron turned to her, his arm across the back of her seat.

"Your grandmother might have gotten disoriented and lost her way," he said. "We'll drive around for a while, maybe we'll get lucky. But Riley, keep in mind—it's dark and it's getting cold. If we don't find her soon, we'll have to call the police in on it."

"I know," she whispered.

He leaned forward and brushed her hair from her forehead. "Maybe it won't come to that," he said. He kissed her on the lips, the pressure as light as a late-season snowfall. "I'm glad you came to me."

Nodding, she fastened her seatbelt, allowing his strength to wash over her.

Aaron drove out of the parking lot and slowly negotiated the roads that ran along the edge of the lake. They rolled the windows down on both sides to better see, and scanned the side streets for headlights or anything else that might be of importance.

Riley's cell phone rang, and she grabbed it.

"Any luck on your end?" Lauren asked.

"No," she said. The momentary hope she'd had that it was her grandmother calling was dashed. "I'm with Aaron. We're driving around on the west side."

"I've called a few of her friends. No one has seen her."

Riley felt the world tilt dangerously again. A dozen possible scenarios raced through her mind, each more frightening than the last. Slowing the SUV to a crawl, Aaron watched Riley as she spoke, his hands on the steering wheel.

"People are starting to wonder what's going on," Lauren added. "I called Bette's friend Joan, who I know has lunch with her a couple of times a month, and Joan has already heard from Vivian at the quilt shop that your grandmother's missing and you're worried."

"Oh, God . . ."

"This is a small town. Word travels fast, especially if the news is bad."

"We don't know the news is bad," Riley said.

"You know what I mean. Even the potential of it is enough to get the speed-dials going full force. At least people are aware we're looking for her, so if—I mean *when*—she's found, they'll know to hang onto her and call you."

"You make her sound like a lost cat," Riley said.

"No, she's the grandmother you love," Lauren said. "She's likely confused and frightened, but you will find her."

"Thanks," Riley murmured.

Aaron picked up speed again, but still kept it slow enough that they could see down each side lane, into every driveway and behind the houses along the way.

They took the occasional turnoff when they thought they'd spotted something, but inevitably it turned out to be the lights of a house deep in the woods around the lake, or something similar. Once it was another car, but, as they drew closer it turned out to be teenagers parked in a picnic area.

They went back to the main road, then took another detour when Aaron thought he saw fresh tracks on an otherwise seldom-used side path. It, too, turned out to be nothing. Along the way they met the occasional car, but none was the one they wanted.

The glowing digital clock on the dashboard read almost nine o'clock.

Riley pulled out her cell phone and called the house. She had to do something, but, as she'd expected, there was no answer.

"It's getting late," Aaron said. "We have to think about bringing the police in on this search."

"I'm not ready to do that yet," Riley said, but her protestations were weak. "Everyone will know something's wrong."

"I think that word is out already."

"I mean about the other . . . the Alzheimer's."

"You can't keep it a secret forever."

"Not forever, I know that, but for a while longer. Think about it, Aaron. Once people know she has Alzheimer's they'll start looking at her in an entirely different way. Any slip of the tongue will be attributed to 'oh, her mind is going.' Her every move will be watched, every innocent blunder blown out of proportion and seen as senility. She'll hate that."

"I suspect people have already noticed something's wrong.

I have, and I see less of her than most of her friends. How many times do you suppose she's gone into the wrong building, or forgotten someone's name, or got lost on her way home? This sort of thing doesn't happen overnight. Just because you're seeing it now for the first time doesn't mean it hasn't already been a topic of speculation."

Riley looked out the window on her side. "I should have picked up on it sooner. I talk to her on the phone every week. Now that I think about it there have been things I noticed, but I brushed them off. If I hadn't closed my eyes to what was going on I might have been able to help her sooner, but I was so wrapped up in my own life that I didn't see what was happening in hers."

"Don't beat yourself up about it. I should have seen that my cousin Hal was having trouble with the restaurant here, but I ignored it until it was almost too late to do anything about it. It's human nature."

"But I should have . . ." Riley's voice cracked, and she was unable to go on.

Aaron reached out a hand and squeezed her knee. "We have to think about finding your grandmother right now. The reality of this situation is that she's out there somewhere, and it's getting damn cold. Do you even know if she took a coat with her?"

"I didn't think to look in the closet," Riley admitted, ashamed.

"All the more reason why we have to find her soon," he stressed. "Before it gets much later. And colder."

Riley dropped her head. Her cell phone, that all-important symbol of modern technology, without which she'd feel as cut off as if she were to lose a limb, was on her lap. She saw it now for what it was—a piece of equipment, a thing that, if she lost it, could be easily replaced.

So much had happened to change her life in a few days. *She* had changed. The outer shell she'd so carefully erected long ago had begun to crumble. Yet, just as she was finding herself, she was losing her grandmother.

"Okay . . . let's call the police," she said. She touched the keypad of her phone with her thumb.

"Wait."

She stopped, and looked at him. Aaron had slowed the vehicle and he was peering intently past her, through the trees, out toward the lake. He brought the SUV to a full stop, then backed up a couple of feet to better see.

"Look at those trees," he said. "Do a couple of them look broken to you? Is there something down there?"

Riley turned. There were few houses in this area, and most of those were cottages that were closed up for the winter. Through the trees the ice glittered on the surface of the lake, reflecting a moon that peeked momentarily out from behind the clouds. "I don't see anything. What are you looking at?"

He sat back. "Nothing. My eyes are starting to go funny." He shifted the SUV into drive and started forward again, then stopped. "I want to take a closer look."

He turned the wheel to the right and edged the vehicle close to the side of the narrow, uneven road. Frozen branches scraped against the side, scratching against the metal like fingernails on a blackboard.

Riley sucked her breath in through her teeth as the front tire dropped into an icy hole and spun. The SUV's 4-while drive kicked in and yanked the tire out, sending them forward with a lurch. Aaron leaned over the steering wheel, his gaze fixed intently on the lake.

"I guess it's nothing . . ." he said.

Leaning almost out of the window on her side, Riley's hands gripped the side of the door. "Wait. What's that?"

Aaron stopped and they saw it at the same time—a faint glow of red on the ice, about forty feet from the shoreline. The clouds overhead parted again and the moon came out.

They saw, in stark detail, the tipped rear end of a vehicle, partially submerged in icy water.

FOURTEEN

Pulling at the door handle on her side, Riley screamed. Aaron was already out. The SUV idled, its front tires buried to the rims in snow. There was a steep, 45-degree drop on the other side of the trees, through thick brush and rocks, thirty or so feet to the lake's edge. Because the beach area here was not optimal for recreation, there were few houses along this stretch of road.

Sliding down the rocky slope, Riley was right behind Aaron as he made his way down through brush and sharp twigs. Aaron didn't wait for her, and she wasn't sure he even knew she was behind him. Near the bottom, she stumbled and fell against him, Aaron turned and grabbed her arm, steadying her.

"Is it her car?" she cried, even though she knew it was. Panic made her voice high and loud.

At the edge of the ice Aaron grabbed her shoulders and stood in front of her. "You stay here," he said, his face pale in the faint glow of moonlight.

She tried to push past him, focused only on getting to her grandmother. Now that they were outside of the SUV, she could feel how very cold it was.

Aaron continued to hold her shoulders tightly. His fingers dug into her arms through the thick parka. "Riley—stop," he commanded. "The ice out there won't hold both of us. Use your cell phone and call 911."

He was right, of course, and she cursed herself for dropping the phone in the SUV. She'd have to climb back up the embankment for it. She looked up, and hesitated.

He gave her a gentle shove in that direction. "Go."

"Be careful," she said over her shoulder, and began to climb.

As she worked her way back up, gripping frost-coated branches with her bare hands, Riley looked down once and saw that Aaron was at the lake's edge. He appeared to be testing the surface of the ice with his boot, leaning his weight forward.

She reached the top and pulled herself over, her knees going through the thin crust of ice on the snow. At the SUV she grabbed her cell phone, which had fallen to the floor.

She punched 911.

"Riley!"

Holding the phone to her ear, she went to the top of the drop-off and saw Aaron far below. He was looking up, and when he saw her he put his hands to the sides of his mouth.

"In the back seat—there's some nylon rope. Bring it down with you," he called.

The emergency operator came on the line. "Nine-one-one. What's the nature of your emergency?"

Riley lifted an arm and waved her understanding to Aaron. Into the phone she said, "There's a car in the lake. It's my grandmother's car—Bette Harrison."

"Is your grandmother in the car?" the operator asked.

Was she? Riley didn't know for sure, but this was not the time to quibble.

"Yes," she said into the phone as she stumbled back to the SUV.

"Where exactly are you located?"

She found a length of yellow nylon rope behind the front seat, coiled like a sleeping snake on the floor. She grabbed it, and noticed at the same time a thick plaid blanket, folded neatly in a square.

Riley pinned the phone against her ear with her shoulder. "On the edge of the lake, the west side I think."

Digging around inside the SUV she also found a flashlight and a pair of gloves. She put the gloves on, and, holding everything else, went back to the edge of the road.

"I need more of a location than that," the operator said.

She held the rope, flashlight and blanket in the crook of her left arm. Holding tightly onto the phone with her right hand, she slid feet-first down the slope, digging in her heels to slow her progress, but still hitting her butt hard against roots and rocks along the way. She ignored the pain.

"Ma'am—at what part of the lake is the car in?" the operator repeated, her voice sounding tiny and distant.

Riley put the phone to her ear again. "Just a minute, I'm not sure."

She got awkwardly to her feet, and hurried to the edge of the lake. On his knees, Aaron was a few feet out on the ice.

"Where are we?" she asked.

"The northwest side of the lake, about half a mile south of the fish hatchery," he said.

Riley repeated this information to the operator.

"Okay, emergency vehicles are on their way out to you," the operator told Riley. "Don't hang up. Stay on the line in case I need to ask you questions."

"All right, but I'm putting the phone down for a minute," Riley said.

"Ma'am—"

She set the phone on the flat surface of a rock, the flip cover open. She carried the rope to the edge of the ice, uncoiled it and threw an end out to Aaron. He caught it, and tied it around his waist. His hands were bare, and she removed the gloves from her own hands.

"Here," she said, and tossed them to him.

Aaron put the gloves on his hands.

Riley picked up the phone again. "I'm back," she told the operator.

With one end of the rope tied around his waist, Aaron lowered himself to his belly and began to crawl out onto the frozen lake. "Tie the other end of the rope around something," he called back to her.

Using the flashlight, Riley looked around. There was plenty of brush and a few saplings, but down here none of the trees looked substantial enough to offer a firm anchor. She finally settled for tying the rope around the base of a sturdy-looking bush, the twigs scraping her hands and digging into her flesh.

Aaron, about fifteen feet out, moved carefully toward the opening in the ice around the car. Riley saw movement inside the vehicle.

Thank God, she thought.

"Gran!" she called. "Stay where you are. Aaron is coming out to you."

She looked up and down the shore both ways. The nearest houses were far in the distance, too far to offer any help. Far-off yard lights offered some faint illumination, but not enough.

The front third of the car was tipped forward through the broken ice at an angle, the headlights at the water's surface, pointing down. Exhaust still pluming from the tailpipe. Inside the vehicle, a dome light came on, and the driver's side door opened a few inches.

"Aaron!" Riley screamed. "She's opening the door."

Aaron's head went up. He continued to crawl forward on his belly, the rope trailing behind like a yellow umbilicus. Looking back over his shoulder, he gauged how far he'd come, and knew it was not far enough. The car was too far away, and he could feel the instability of the ice beneath him. It creaked and shifted like a thing alive with his every movement, protesting against his weight, threatening him with an icy plunge at any moment. By lying down he'd distributed his weight more evenly over a greater area, but he didn't know if that would be enough to keep him from breaking through.

He looked ahead again and saw the driver's-side door opening. Water rushed into the car through the gap, weighing down the interior of the vehicle, which sank a couple of inches deeper.

"Close the door, Bette!" he shouted. "I'm coming out to you."

If she heard, she gave no indication, and the door remained ajar. The headlights were now halfway below water level, their glow casting an eerie radiance into the ink-black water. Through the rear window of the car Aaron could see the faint outline of a figure, and occasional movement.

He slid forward a few more inches, then stopped, holding his breath, when the ice crackled and moaned. He moved forward again—slowly, so slowly it felt as though he was making no progress at all. His ears strained for the sound of ambulance or police sirens. If this ice gave out, both he and

Bette would need the services of emergency personnel very quickly.

Riley paced back and forth at the edge of the lake, her boots crunching on the snow, the blanket clutched in her arms. She also listened for sirens, willing help to arrive. She felt powerless, unable to do anything more and frustrated by the slowness of Aaron's progress. Why didn't he move faster?

At her feet the rope shifted, unwinding a little more, an indication that he was making progress, however sluggish it might be. She stared at the rope. Her eyes went back out to Aaron, spread-eagle on the ice, and the car—still a distance in front of him.

She looked back down at the rope, and a new realization dawned.

He was not going to have enough rope to reach the sinking car.

Sweeping at the wood shavings on his kitchen floor, Fitz Fitzpatrick cleaned up the remnants of an ongoing project. He was working on a hand-carved chess set for his nephew's graduation, and he'd just finished a pawn, three inches high and carved from a block of oak. It was a fine piece. He was happy with the way the project was coming along, and, thinking about the next piece he would work on, Fitz only half-listened to the scanner on his kitchen counter as he swept.

The scanner sputtered with static as he bent and brushed the shavings into a dustpan. Lots of people kept scanners. It was snooping, he knew, but he liked the immediacy of knowing what was happening in and around town. Besides regular updates on the weather, he heard the police reports, ambulance calls, all kinds of useful information. Codes were used for a lot of the calls, but he'd been listening long enough that he'd figured out what the codes meant, with some help from another nephew, who was on the fire department.

The static on the scanner intensified as Fitz dumped the shavings into the garbage bin, and a voice came over the radio.

". . . emergency crew is on its way to the location . . ."

It was a callout on a car that had gone through the ice in

the lake. Fitz leaned on the end of his broom to listen, interested but not alarmed by the report. Cars fell through the ice now and then. Usually it was one of those fool ice-fishermen. They drove their cars out onto the lake during the deep-cold months, but they were supposed to pay attention to the thickness of the ice and behave accordingly. Later in the season, as the water temperature dropped and the ice began to thaw, it would no longer support the weight of a vehicle.

If a car did go through the ice, and subsequently sank to the bottom of the lake, the unfortunate owner would not only lose his car to the destructive nature of the water, he'd also pay a hefty fee to have it retrieved. Fitz had heard once that it could cost thousands of dollars for a retrieval company to pull a car from the bottom of the lake. Leaving it there wasn't an option. The oil and gasoline were pollutants that couldn't be allowed to stay.

". . . car went off the road onto the ice . . ."

Fitz listened to the report hoping the owner of the vehicle would be named. With any luck it would be one of his cronies, someone he could mercilessly rib for months to come—assuming, of course, no one got hurt.

Crackle, crackle. ". . . the location is Old Mill Road, south of the fish hatchery."

Fitz new the area. It was a few miles from where he lived.

A second voice came through. "Do we have a name on the occupants?"

"One occupant. The car in question belongs to a local resident, Bette Harrison. It sounds like she's in it."

"On our way."

More static.

Fitz dropped his broom. He was out of the kitchen, grabbing for his coat and car keys before the broom hit the linoleum. He raced out the front door and to his pickup, which was parked by the front porch. Tires spinning, he headed for Old Mill Road.

Aaron was chilled to the bone, the ice beneath him having penetrated through his clothing long ago. He wasn't dressed for a belly-crawl on solid ice. The gloves Riley had tossed him were inadequate, and his fingers felt stiff and unresponsive within them.

At a tug on the line that tethered him to the shore, he looked carefully back over his shoulder, trying not to disturb the unstable ice. The shoreline was well behind him now and he saw Riley there, a small figure in a red parka, her face a white oval. She was shouting at him, one hand encircling the yellow nylon line.

"There's not enough rope!" she called, holding the line up so that he could see it had reached the last coil.

Aaron's heart sank at the sight of that diminishing line. He needed at least ten more feet to reach the car. Looking forward again, he saw the car shift a few inches. The headlights were now entirely underwater, the rear tilted higher. The front-heavy vehicle was being pulled slowly but inexorably into the water.

Riley had called for help. He wondered if he could wait where he was and hope it would arrive soon. A rescue crew would have more line, and hooks to attach to the back bumper of the car to keep it from slipping farther below the surface while they got Bette out. He hesitated, listening for the sound of distant sirens.

He heard nothing but the crack of the ice beneath him as it protested his weight.

The door of the vehicle opened a few inches more, and the frightened face of Bette Harrison peered out at him.

"Stay still!" he called out to her, waving one arm. "Help is coming."

Bette continued to push the door until it was stopped about halfway by the edge of the ice. She looked down into the swirling water, then back at Aaron. One foot appeared as she started to climb out of the car.

Riley watched with growing horror as her grandmother began to work her way through the half-open car door, her every movement making the vehicle shift unsteadily.

"Gran, don't!" she shouted from the shore. "Aaron, stop her!"

Stepping out onto the ice, Riley wanted to rush out there

herself, to run to her grandmother and bring her safely back to shore. But two steps was all it took, and the ice creaked beneath her boots. She thought about getting down to redistribute her weight, as Aaron had done, but sanity prevailed and she knew to go out there would endanger them all. She backed up, frustrated and frightened, daring to go no farther.

She looked down at the blanket on the ground. "Aaron, wait!" she called.

Bending down, she untied the end of the rope from the base of the bush, and, with cold-stiffened fingers, managed to tie one corner of the blanket to the rope. She stepped to the edge of the ice and held tightly onto the opposite corner of the blanket. The improvised tether added about five feet of length. Aaron crept forward a little farther.

Halfway out of the car now, Bette put her shoe on the ice, one bare hand gripping the top of the door. Where her shoe tested the ice the water was already churning, rising higher and seeping into the car, adding weight that would make it sink even quicker.

Aaron didn't waste any more breath shouting at her. All he wanted to do now was get to her, and hopefully grab onto her before she tumbled into the bitterly cold water. Maybe the ice would hold them both. Maybe.

As Bette put more weight down on the ice, her shoe sank into the water. She cried out at the sudden cold, but instead of retreating back to the temporary safety of the car, she continued coming out.

Aaron grew desperate. He was less than five feet from the rear of the car now, but he could see clearly that the broken edge of the ice would not hold Bette once she put her full weight on it. And his hands felt so frozen that he had the new fear that, even if he reached her in time, he wouldn't be able to hang onto her. If she panicked, she might drag them both down.

The ice beneath his chest cracked alarmingly, and web-like gaps spread out on both sides as he felt it sink. He stopped, praying the ice would hold. It did—for the moment. He pushed himself forward a few more inches.

He was four feet from the rear bumper of the car, but here the ice was even more treacherous. Daring to look back over his shoulder, he hoped that help might have arrived. Only Riley stood on the edge of the frozen lake.

Three feet. The rope pulled tight around his waist. He was again out of line.

With an outstretched arm he could nearly touch one of the back tires, which had come up several inches off the ice as the front sank lower.

Bette was almost out of the car. She clung to the open door with both hands, her body angled toward him, both feet on the sinking ice. The water was up to her mid-calf, and her expression was terrified.

He couldn't reach her. Knowing what he had to do, Aaron untied the rope from around his waist. Free of the restriction, he reached out with his right hand and gripped the raised bumper. There was no point in trying to stop her. The best he could hope for now was that the ice would hold long enough for her to reach him. He extended his left hand to her.

"Bette, come this way," he implored.

She looked at him, and a flicker of hope danced over her features. She released the door long enough to reach out to him.

"Get down low, like me," he instructed.

She nodded. The simple gesture, an indication of awareness, filled Aaron with renewed hope. But the ice he was on was breaking away, the black water rising up so that now it nearly touched him. The spider's-web cracks widened, spreading open as they gave up to the onslaught of weight and water.

Bette's hand was inches from Aaron's as she lowered herself down to her knees. She was wearing slacks, and as her knees touched the ice it dipped farther below the surface so the water was up to her thighs. She cried out, startled by the cold, but continued to move toward him.

Their fingers were almost touching. Aaron stretched out as far as he could, hanging onto the bumper as the only solid thing that might support them.

Riley watched from the shore, pacing back and forth, still holding the end of the blanket even though Aaron had freed himself of the rope. She held her breath as her grandmother crouched down low, and seemed almost to reach him.

Then, as Riley watched, the ice gave way completely and they both plunged into the deep, black water.

Fitz came up behind the ambulance at the fish hatchery turn, and he followed it from that point on.

Ahead of the ambulance he could see a police car, both vehicles with their lights flashing and sirens going. Despite the layer of ice on the curving road they maintained a lurching speed that he wouldn't have dared try on his own, but behind the ambulance he kept up, his body hunched over the steering wheel as he struggled to maintain control of his car. The last thing anyone needed was for him to go off the road, too. Bad enough having to pull one car out of the lake, if he added a second he'd just as soon sink than face the humiliation of being fished out.

But he couldn't bring himself to slow down. From the moment he'd heard Bette's name on the scanner, that she was in her car and it had gone through the ice, Fitz had been unable to slow down.

For the past couple of months he'd been looking for any excuse to spend time with Bette. He'd even joined the genealogy club, an interest he hadn't previously had, as a way to be near her. He'd admired Bette Harrison for a long time, but had considered her a casual friend and nothing more. Not until after Joe Harrison had passed away a few years ago, and then Fitz's own wife, Leonore, a year ago, had he begun to see Bette in a new light. Thoughts of a late-in-life romance had begun to form in his mind, and he'd angled for any opportunity to bask in the sunlight of her quick laughter and sharp mind. And that's what was breaking his heart lately, because he recognized the signs. Leonore, his wife of almost forty-five years, had suffered the ravages of Alzheimer's during the last three years of her life. He'd witnessed her deterioration daily, until he'd begun to wish for an end to the indignities of a mind that was gone, and a body that was a shell of its former self.

When he'd begun to notice similar lapses in Bette he'd wondered, briefly, if he could stand to go through that again. He'd thought about saving himself, of walking away from the heartbreak to come, but in the end he'd been unable to do so. Instead, he'd begun to take over in little ways. When he saw her struggling to remember a name, he'd casually slip it in, without bringing attention to her forgetfulness. He'd begun taking her for her weekly grocery shopping, always using the excuse that it was he who needed help in deciding which laundry detergent to buy, or how to choose the best fruits and vegetables. During these outings he quietly kept an eye on her, making sure her own list was in order, and that she didn't double up on items. He'd also been able to protect her somewhat at their genealogy meetings. None of the other members realized yet that she sometimes lost her notes, or forgot previously familiar sites. The charade couldn't last forever, he knew, but he'd hoped he could put off the inevitable for a bit longer.

He held the steering wheel tightly, his eyes on the ambulance directly ahead. To lose Bette now, while she still had some quality of life left, would be a cruelty Fitz didn't want to contemplate.

Riley screamed when she saw Aaron and her grandmother tumble into the water. Again she tested the ice, and again she was forced to retreat when she felt its instability. The only thing that kept her from a suicidal plunge forward was the sound of approaching sirens.

She wound the end of the blanket around the bush and scrambled up the embankment to the SUV. She stood in the middle of the road and waved her arms, signaling to the approaching vehicles. A police car pulled up, followed closely by an ambulance, then, not far behind, another car. Riley ran to the ambulance just as two male emergency medical technicians were getting out.

"They fell in the water!" she shouted, pointing in the direction of the lake.

The EMTs opened the back doors of the ambulance, and a

woman got out, pulling equipment with her. "How many people?" the female EMT asked.

"Two. My grandmother, Bette Harrison, and Aaron Wolfe. He went out to try to help her, but they both fell in."

"How long ago did they go in the water?"

"It just happened."

Two police officers emerged from their car, flashlights in hand. They began working their way down the embankment.

A big truck rumbled in from the opposite direction, turned, and backed up close to the edge of the drop-off. On the side door was painted the words, Okoboji Water Rescue, and in its rear bed was what looked like a giant spool, around which was· wound a thick cable.

"Good, the rescue truck is here," the female EMT said.

"What's that for?" Riley asked.

"We'll send a cable down to attach to the car. That'll stabilize it so it doesn't sink."

One of the male EMTs went down the embankment, while the other went to the newly arrived rescue truck.

A figure appeared at Riley's side.

"Riley, what's going on?" Fitz asked. "How did Bette's car get in the lake?"

She shook her head, not taking the time to wonder at his arrival. "I don't know how it all started. I have to get down there."

For the third time she slid down the ice and snow-covered slope to the lake, leaving Fitz behind.

The cold water had hit Aaron like a fist, knocking the wind from his lungs and almost immediately paralyzing his limbs. Somehow, though, he managed to grab Bette's shirt just as they'd both gone into the water. At first they both went below the surface, but he fought his way back to the edge of the ice, with her in tow, within a few seconds. Those few seconds were enough. Aaron felt as though most of the strength had been sapped from his limbs, and his muscles cramped painfully.

Bette gasped for air as he held her above water, sometimes to his own detriment. Looking around for what remained of the car, he hoped to find something there to loop an arm over, but the only part of the car within reach was the ice-coated side. Halfway below the surface now, the car was making its slow, inevitable way into the lake, and creating a new fear— once it went all the way in, it might just suck them down with it if they were too weak to stay above the surface.

With frozen fingers, his gloves a soggy, useless mess, Aaron tried to grab the edge of the ice. It slipped away from him. Blinking against the biting cold, he saw movement at the lake's edge and realized help had at last arrived. That sight helped him rally his strength, and kept him from slipping down into the beckoning water.

Using the last of his reserves, Aaron pushed Bette around in front of him. Earlier she'd been filled with panic, but now she was lethargic from the cold, her lips blue, eyes closed. He pushed her arms up onto the edge of the ice. He saw the end of the rope lying there, and he was just able to grab it and bring it to them. There wasn't enough of it to tie around anything, but he put the end into Bette's hands and forced her fingers closed around it.

"Try to hang on," he urged, wondering how much longer he would be able to hold her. But if he went below the surface again, he wanted her to at least have a chance.

She didn't react to his plea. She neither opened her eyes nor made any attempt to hold onto the rope. Only her shallow, labored breathing gave any indication that she was still alive.

Aaron gave her a shove up, hoping to put the upper half of her body onto the ice. All it did was force him down, and he gulped in a mouthful of freezing water as his head went underwater. He came up sputtering, but was gratified to see that Bette was now making an effort to hold onto the rope. She lay with her upper arms on the smooth surface of the ice, her cheek resting on one soaked sleeve. Her eyes were still closed, but her breathing seemed less labored.

He didn't know how much longer he'd be able to keep his head above water.

Behind him Aaron could feel the pull of the car as it continued its slow downward slide. The water swirled around him, sucking at his clothing. He continued to tread water, not wanting to grab the ice again in case he broke off the chunk on which Bette rested. He could do nothing but try to relax, hoping his natural buoyancy would keep him afloat for a while, but feeling the heavy pull of his saturated clothing and boots as they weighed him down. He thought of removing his boots, then dismissed the idea. Without them he might easier keep afloat, but he couldn't risk further exposing his frozen feet. Besides, he didn't think his fingers would manage the job of unlacing the ties even if he wanted to.

Tilting his chin up in an effort to keep his mouth above water, Aaron looked at the inky sky above. It was dotted with stars, some clouds, and a moon that looked down impassively on their plight.

He could hear shouting from the shore, but he dared not look. Every ounce of strength he had left he needed to keep his face above water. As it was, he could feel himself growing heavier by the moment, his limbs less responsive as hypothermia set it. In this temperature hypothermia could prove deadly in minutes, though most victims ended up drowning as the muscles in their extremities locked up and they sank into the water.

He thought about Riley. Closing his eyes for a moment, he pictured her deep chestnut hair, and the way it smelled when he'd held her in his arms. He'd wanted to bury himself in that hair, to catch its tangles in his fingers, the scent, lemony from the shampoo she used, already familiar to him. Her hair was silken fire, and the thought of it was almost warming, a comforting blaze to heat and soothe his tortured muscles.

The memory of their brief time together at his house, their limbs entwined, sustained him. At the time he'd thought they would have more of those evenings together. It had seemed so natural to hold her, as though their bodies were made for each other, the ease with which the curves and angles fit together a promise of future joinings. He'd marveled at the smooth, lightly freckled quality of her skin, the faint golden tan that spoke of her Texas home, fading already under the pale Iowa sun.

She'd sighed softly as he'd brushed his lips across the smooth slope of her breasts—not really a kiss, but a contact that spoke deeper than that. He'd tasted her skin, the saltiness in the hollow of her throat, felt the vibration there almost like the contented purr of a cat.

Eyes closed, Aaron smiled at the memory.

The water no longer seemed uncomfortable. It welcomed him . . . a deep, engulfing bed that would be so easy to slip down into . . .

Fitz watched from atop the embankment, where he had a clear view of the goings-on below. One of the EMTs had inflated a wide rubber raft. The cable on the rescue truck had a two-foot hook on the end, which one of the men had dragged down to the dinghy. The rescuers had taken the time to don wetsuits, undoubtedly a precaution against the cold water in case they also fell in, but the precious time it had all taken had sent Fitz into a torment of frustration.

A small crowd had begun to gather around him—the third EMT, and two more police officers who'd come up in yet another cruiser. There were also now at least two more cars and the people who'd gotten out of them, perhaps drawn by the news on their scanners, as he'd been, but more likely they'd been driving by and had seen the excitement.

"Who's out there?" a female voice beside Fitz asked.

He turned and saw a woman who he knew as a waitress from the coffee shop he sometimes went to for lunch. Her name, he remembered, was Bethany. She was still wearing her uniform under a navy pea coat, and she shivered as she pulled it closer around herself.

"It's Bette Harrison's car," he told her, a composure to his voice he didn't feel. "And that's Bette and Aaron Wolfe out there."

"No kidding," she said. She crossed herself, then moved past him to get a better look at the rescue attempt. "How'd they get out there?"

"I don't know," he said, and offered nothing more.

A couple had also appeared to watch the activity below. "I heard people were looking for Bette earlier," the woman said. "That she was lost or something."

Her husband, chubby and balding, craned his neck. His face, like his wife's, was expressionless, as though the excitement below was nothing more than a movie flickering on a theater screen. All they needed was a box of popcorn. "Isn't that her granddaughter down there, the one that's visiting?" he asked his wife.

"Yeah, that's her. I saw her at the park a couple of days ago."

"Hey!" Bethany gasped. "I think Aaron just went under!"

FIFTEEN

Riley watched from the edge of the lake as the little inflatable dinghy, tethered to the shore with yet another line, slid easily over the ice. One of the rubber-clad emergency workers pushed it while the other sat in the boat with the cable-held hook. The boat's wide, flat bottom kept the weight evenly distributed, and as they neared the edge of the broken ice the man in the boat expertly threw the hook, which caught on the back bumper of the car. The cable tightened and held. The car, which had been inching deeper into the water, jerked to a stop.

Floodlights had been set up, which illuminated the surface of the lake with a faint, ghostly glow. The second rescuer scrambled into the dinghy, and both men reached far out on the other side. For a moment it looked as though they might tumble into the water themselves. But they didn't, and when they pulled back they were hauling Bette into the boat.

A cheer went up from the people gathered at the top of the embankment. There were several there now, as well as more on the snow-packed shore.

Riley sobbed with relief at the sight of her grandmother being brought to safety. She couldn't see beyond the dinghy, but one of the EMTs was leaning over on the far side again, stretching for something that seemed just out of his reach. The other EMT, looking back toward shore, waved his arms high over his head.

The female EMT, the one who'd stayed with their transport vehicle, slid down the embankment and moved to Riley's side at the edge of the lake. Holding a walkie-talkie in her hand, she spoke into it. "Do you see him? Can you grab him?"

The walkie-talkie crackled. "Can't see . . . think we lost him."

Riley felt a moan rise from deep within her, as though the icy water had washed over her, as well. "No . . ." she begged. "Don't lose him."

The EMT said, "Can you get a light on him?"

Crackle. "Wait . . . is that him? Throw him a line."

Another voice. "He can't hang onto it."

There was a flurry of excited movement around Riley, but she saw none of it. The police officers had also come to help with the floodlights, and to keep people from gathering too close to the edge of the ice. Riley paced back and forth in hand-wringing distress, the frenetic activity on and around the lake corresponding with the churning turmoil she felt within.

Aaron had gone out there to save her grandmother. If anything happened to him as a result, the guilt would haunt her for the rest of her life. But, more than that, she also saw the true emptiness of a life without him. To lose him now, just as she was beginning to find it within herself to open up and offer her heart to another person, would be a blow too crushing to endure.

She took a step closer to the ice, forgetting the danger, wanting only to be out there.

The walkie-talkie again squawked. *Crackle.* ". . . think we got him. Wait . . . yeah, hang on."

Out on the lake, the men in the dinghy leaned far over the side of their craft, tugging at something just beyond sight. They straightened, straining with the effort. Their grunts of exertion could be heard all the way to the shore.

Then Riley saw what they had—Aaron, wet and limp, being pulled into the boat.

Another cheer went up from the ever-increasing crowd, and Riley felt her knees hit the snow as her legs, no longer able to support her, gave out. Someone put a hand on her arm as though to help her up, but she shook her head. She needed to stay down for a moment as she fought the lightheadedness that swept over her.

She raised her eyes long enough to watch as they lifted Aaron the rest of the way into the boat. Then the EMTs signaled to be pulled back to shore. Several sets of hands grabbed the rope that was tethered to the little boat, and it began its slow return to the shore.

A microphone was shoved close to Riley's face.

"Are you a relative of the people in the car?" a young man asked. In his mid or late twenties, he had the bright, earnest expression of a youthful reporter, still new enough to the job to be excited about the news he covered.

Riley blinked up at him as though he'd just stepped from a spacecraft. A badge clipped to his parka indicated he was with the local radio station. She looked up the hill, and saw a white van with the station's call letters on the side.

Word of trouble gets out fast in a small town.

Shaking her head, she slapped the microphone away, and returned her gaze to the small rescue boat. It was now only a few feet from shore. Several people were busy pulling it in, and as it reached the edge of the ice one of the EMTs hopped out.

Riley got to her feet and pushed through the dozen or so onlookers, making her way to the boat. Her grandmother was sitting up, wrapped in blankets but alert and shivering. Aaron lay still on the bottom of the boat while the other EMT leaned over him.

Reluctantly, Riley dragged her worried eyes away from Aaron and turned to her grandmother. "Oh, Gran," she cried. She would have crawled into the boat if a police officer hadn't stopped her.

"Stay back," he said, his voice firm. "Let us help them."

"She's my grandmother."

"Riley," Bette said weakly. She lifted a trembling hand.

The EMT helped Bette to her feet, then assisted her out of the boat. Riley enveloped her grandmother in a hug, relief flooding through her despite the worries that still lingered. "It's going to be all right," she said softly, her cheek close to the older woman's. "I won't leave you, Gran. I promise."

Bette tightened her hold on Riley briefly, then exhaustion took over and she slumped forward. One of the officers grabbed her before she went over entirely. The two male EMTs, along with another policeman, were working on Aaron. Riley was aware of this, but she couldn't bring herself to look over there. As much as the cold fear for him knifed through her, her first responsibility was to her grandmother.

"We have to get her up to the ambulance," the female EMT told Riley.

It was obvious Bette would not be able to make the climb up to the road on her own. Yet another line lowered a gurney, and the female EMT, with the help of the officers, eased Bette into it. They strapped her securely in, and more people pitched in to help get the gurney up the steep incline.

Riley scrambled up the hill behind them.

They put Bette in the back of the ambulance, and the female EMT began working to remove her wet clothing. Riley helped, even as a part of her mind stayed down at the edge of the lake, with Aaron.

Bette was shivering violently. When Riley expressed concern, the EMT said, "No, that's good. It's the body's way of warming her up. I'd be a lot more worried if she *weren't* shivering."

Bette's eyes fluttered open. "Riley," she whispered. "Did I fall down the stairs?"

"You were in the car," Riley told her. "Do you remember anything about the accident?"

Frowning, Bette shook her head. "In the car? What was I doing in the car?"

"You were going to the store. You must have gotten lost."

"No . . . I know every road around this town, I wouldn't get lost here." But she sounded uncertain, and a flicker of fear shadowed her expression.

"You're going to be all right," Riley said, her voice choked with emotion. She held her grandmother's hand. It was cold and stiff, but the older woman managed to give a feeble, responsive squeeze.

A flash of lucidity replaced the fear in Bette's eyes. "What's going to happen now? How will I take care of things?"

"Don't worry about that."

"I have to. The cabins, the business . . ."

"No, Gran, you don't have to worry, I promise. I'm going to stay and make sure everything is okay." But even as Riley spoke the words to allay her grandmother's fears, she wondered how long she could really remain.

Bette settled back on the cot, and Riley moved out of the

way so the EMT could do her job. The EMT placed a warming blanket over Bette, her movements efficient yet gentle.

A concerned, weathered face peeked in through the open back doors of the ambulance.

"How is she?" Fitz asked.

Riley hadn't noticed him among the crush of onlookers when Bette had been brought up to the ambulance. Now she exhaled, glad to see a familiar face. "I think she's going to be okay . . . for the most part," she said, keeping her words deliberately vague.

There were sounds of more activity outside. Riley got up and leaned out to see what was going on. Fitz also turned.

Several people were pulling the gurney over the edge of embankment. It contained the unmoving, still-dripping form of Aaron Wolfe.

"He was in the water a long time," Fitz observed, reaching out a hand to help Riley from the ambulance.

"No, it was just a few minutes," she said, more to reassure herself than anything. She took his hand, but once her feet were on the ground she found she could go no farther. She was afraid to move, afraid of what she would see when she looked into Aaron's face, afraid of the news she would receive.

"A few minutes is a long time when you're talking sub-freezing temps," Fitz said.

Now that she knew her grandmother was out of immediate danger, Riley allowed herself to think about Aaron. Her mind, however, would take her only so far into that treacherous territory. When she contemplated the darker possibilities, she felt faint with dread.

"I can walk." The familiar voice was weak, but held an underlying note of spirited rebellion.

Riley gasped.

"Sounds like he's going to make it," Fitz said.

Riley rushed to the side of the embankment. The EMTs there were wrestling with Aaron, who struggled to sit up in the gurney.

"Lay down and let us get you into the ambulance," one of them ordered.

Aaron tried to lift one booted foot over the side. "Let me

out of this thing," he growled.

Riley reached his side and threw herself at him, knocking him back onto the gurney. He grunted with surprise, then wrapped an ice-encrusted arm around her. "Babe, you look good," he said in her ear.

He was shivering, even more so than Bette had been, and even as he continued to insist he could make his way to the ambulance on his own, he fell back in exhaustion.

Riley clung to him. He was drenched, his clothes stiff with a thin layer of ice, but she didn't care. He was alive, with a semblance of his old, stubborn self showing through, and at the moment that was all that mattered to her. "I thought I'd lost you," she said, her tears hot against the wet slab of ice that was his cheek.

"No chance of that. How's your grandmother?"

"She's good, thanks to you. Oh, Aaron... you saved her life. She would have gone under before the paramedics reached her. But I couldn't have stood it if I'd lost you in the process."

His expression brightened. "Really? Red, I think that's the nicest thing you've ever said to me."

"Don't call me Red." She sniffled, smiling, and allowed the EMTs to pull her away from him.

The crowd began to break up as Aaron was loaded into the back of the ambulance with Bette. Only Fitz continued to hover nearby, the concern so evident in his expression that Riley promised him she would call from the hospital as soon as she had anything more to report.

She drove the SUV, following the ambulance that took Aaron and her grandmother to the hospital.

In a drug-induced sleep, Bette looked almost young again, as though in rest the years' accumulation of work, worry and just plain living had temporarily fled her features. The doctors had administered a sedative to ensure she'd get a good night's rest. Riley, however, had received no such consolation. Sitting beside her grandmother's bed, she felt heavy with exhaustion. She rubbed at her eyes, then pushed herself to her feet, afraid that if she continued to sit she'd end up falling over onto the floor. She stood at her grandmother's bedside for a moment, then pulled the edge of the blanket up and tucked it in around her shoulders. Certain that her grandmother wouldn't wake up until morning, Riley walked down the hallway, to the room in which she knew Aaron rested.

She found him sitting up, quarreling with two nurses. He'd already swung one leg out from under the covers, while the nurses tried to prevent him from leaping out of the bed.

"You're going to stay overnight for observation," said one of the nurses, a no-nonsense woman who looked strong enough to hold him down if it came to that. Her name tag said Karolyn G, RN. "You had a close call, Mr. Wolfe—we need to be sure you're completely well before you go running off."

"I'll be completely well when I'm out of here and in my own bed," Aaron argued. "Haven't you read the latest reports? Patients recover faster in their home environment."

"*When* they are well enough to go home," Nurse Karolyn said, pushing him back. "Your core body temperature isn't all the way up to where it's supposed to be. Until you register 98.6 you'll stay here for observation."

"How do you know it's not 98.6 right now? It's been at least an hour since anyone checked."

"Not enough time has passed. However, if you insist, I'll be glad to take your temperature again—rectally this time, just to be sure."

Aaron snarled at her, his eyes narrowed with displeasure.

The other nurse, young enough to be barely out of school, hovered nervously nearby.

"Toni, get the rectal thermometer," Nurse Karolyn ordered.

The young nurse's eyes widened, but she made a move to comply.

"Wait," Aaron snapped. He stopped struggling, his arms crossed over his chest. "Okay, forget it. But I want it noted that I'm staying here under protest."

"Oh, we'll note that, no doubt about it."

Riley, who'd watched this exchange from the safety of the doorway, stepped into the room as the nurses left. "Don't stay long," the nurse said as she moved past Riley.

"She'll stay as long as I want her to," Aaron called after

them. Then he slumped back on the bed, arms still crossed, his brows drawn together in a severe frown. "I think all nurses go to Nazi training school as part of their degree requirement. Couple of bullies. But the young one was kind of cute."

Riley leaned over and kissed his cheek. "You may have scared her out of the nursing profession. So you think she's cute, huh?"

Aaron brightened. "Not as cute as you. God, you look good." He put his arms around her and pulled her in. "Can't you spring me from this place?"

Wobbly with fatigue, and a delayed crash from the adrenaline rush she'd had earlier, Riley leaned into him to absorb some of his strength. She ached everywhere, though she wasn't sure what she'd done, other than pace back and forth at the edge of the lake, to make her body hurt so much. She felt as though she'd run a triathlon—and had come out badly.

"I think you should listen to your doctors," she said. "They have your best interest in mind."

"Oh, so you're on their side." But when he pulled back he was smiling. "I'm going to repeat what I just said—you look good."

"I couldn't possibly," Riley said. She'd looked in a mirror minutes earlier, in her grandmother's room. Her hair was stringy and her face was colorless except for the dark circles beneath he eyes. She'd probably never looked worse.

"You always look good to me. The first time I saw you, there in the coffee shop, I knew you were a woman I wanted to get to know."

"Did you really?"

"Absolutely. Of course, I never expected you'd become such a big part of my life so quickly, but there it is—one of life's happy surprises."

Riley let her eyes drift over him, her exhaustion giving way to something deeper—a longing she hadn't known she could feel. She wanted to love this man. She *did* love this man, she realized, the ache of it filling her heart until she thought it would burst. But how could she allow herself to think about loving Aaron when, first and foremost, she had to figure out what she was going to do about her grandmother? It wasn't right to put the rest of her life on hold, she knew that, and she also knew her grandmother wouldn't want it, but she had an obligation to the one person who'd always been there for her. If that meant putting her job, her personal life, everything else on a back burner for now, then that's what she'd do.

"Get some rest," she whispered. "I'll come back to see you in the morning."

"You're leaving?"

"Gran's out for the night, they gave her something to help her rest. I'm going to the house to get some sleep."

"Hey, I'm being selfish, aren't I?" he said. "It's a bad habit of mine, or so I've been told. Go home and get some sleep. You can come back and have hospital-food breakfast with me in the morning. Then I *am* leaving this joint, and no one's going to stop me."

"I have a feeling they won't try."

SIXTEEN

Her bed beckoned, and Riley expected to fall on it and pass out in sheer exhaustion. Instead, she found she was unable to turn off the turmoil in her head. She lay there on her back, looking up at the ceiling, until she couldn't stand it any longer and she got up and went to her laptop.

She turned it on and stared at the screen. There was a new e-mail from Emily, sent later in the day, after Riley had spoken to Joel. He must have worked some of his magic, because the tone of Emily's latest missive was less hostile than she'd sounded earlier. Sitting back, Riley wondered why she didn't feel more relieved. She knew she could still go back and smooth things over with Emily. They'd had a good working relationship over the years. It was unlikely anything drastic would happen to Riley's career with the company over the problems of these past few days. But what she mostly felt about it, she realized, was indifference.

There was a problem with some of the websites? Big deal. One of her co-workers was trying to undermine her work? To hell with it.

Riley closed the e-mail and shut down the computer.

Her eyes drifted to the partial document, which she'd been so concerned about earlier, on the desk next to her computer. She picked it up and carried it downstairs, still in her cotton pajamas. In the kitchen she poured herself a glass of milk, and took it and the papers to the sofa in the family room. She'd have to ask her grandmother again if she remembered anything about this, but Riley hated to nag her about it, especially in light of what Bette had just been through. Or she could tear the house apart looking for the rest of it, but either way there was nothing more that could be done tonight.

Sipping her milk, she thought again about Aaron. She

knew she had to confront the possibility that he might've had something to do with this. Was he trying to buy her grandmother's property? If so, it would have taken place before Riley got here, so she couldn't claim it indicated any disloyalty to her. Would his new relationship with her over these past few days change any plans he might've made? There was no longer any way Riley could tell herself this thing she had going with Aaron was just a fling. The situation was much more complicated than that, culminating with her recent realization that she loved Aaron Wolfe. In a few short days this man had worked his way into her heart like no one else ever had, to the point where the thought of losing him—out there on the lake— had dropped her to her knees in grief.

She loved him, wanted him, needed him—but did she entirely trust him? He was ambitious, buying up property around the lake, always with an eye on building it up and increasing its value. And his profits. She didn't fault him for having an entrepreneurial spirit. That sharpness, that clarity of vision, was one of the things about him she'd found attractive in the first place. But would his ambition lead him to take advantage of a confused old woman?

The papers in her hand felt poisonous with dark meaning, and until she knew who the instigator of the document was, that venomous doubt would remain in her mind. She was going to have to ask Aaron flat-out. She knew this, but she also dreaded it. What if he *had* tricked her grandmother into signing away her property? Even if done before he'd gotten to know Riley, it would still contaminate everything between them.

A new thought occurred to her. What if Aaron had deliberately cozied up to her this week to find out what she knew about the document, and about his attempts to buy the resort? *That* scenario was one Riley didn't even want to contemplate, and one that, deep down, she didn't really believe. Her instincts told her he wasn't that duplicitous.

Setting her glass down on the end table, she turned off the lamp. Her head felt stuffed with cotton, and her eyelids drooped.

She didn't want to think, analyze or question any more

tonight. It was almost two a.m. She needed her rest for what lay ahead. Her grandmother was going to need her here, for how long Riley had no idea. But she did know she'd be useless to herself or anyone else if she didn't find some respite from her own gloomy thoughts.

Yawning, she reached for a throw pillow and arranged it under her head as she lay on the sofa.

Her eyes opened with a jerk. She'd dozed after all, but had been startled awake by something. What . . . a dream?

No. A sound.

She heard it again, and sat up. It had come from outside, faint and distant enough that if her nerves hadn't been already seriously rattled she might have slept through it. It had come from the direction of the cabins, and even in sleep her subconscious had distinguished the diffcrence between this new noise and the normal nocturnal sounds.

Riley got up, and immediately felt how much more her muscles had stiffened up in just this short time. At the front door she put her parka on over her pajamas, and pushed her feet back into the boots that had served her so well lately. She opened the door without turning on the porch light. The laces of the boots trailed behind her as she stepped lightly down the front steps, turned right and looked at the double row of cabins less than twenty yards away.

There was a light showing through the window of one of the cabins. It cut through the dark, fading in and out as it moved. Riley recognized it as the beam of a flashlight. There was someone inside Purple Martin.

She looked around. Aaron's SUV, which she'd driven home from the hospital and put in the garage, was out of sight. Her own rental car was still at the restaurant. The light fabric of her pajamas didn't offer much protection, even with the parka. Riley shivered in the cold night air, but she moved ahead, watching her steps as she went so as not to give the intruder advance warning.

She wondered about going back to the house and calling 911, but dismissed the idea as hasty. Besides, she'd had enough of emergency services for one night. All she wanted for the moment was a peek at whoever was in the cabin. Then she'd deal with it tomorrow.

The light inside the window continued to move in sweeping arcs. There was a soft thud from within the cabin. The front door was ajar a few inches, and she put one hand on the doorframe to peer through the opening.

A figure moved about in the shadows. Riley's eyes adjusted to the gloom, and with the aid of the still-moving flashlight beam she saw that a chair had been overturned. Pillows had been thrown about the room, and there was a deep tear in a sofa cushion, as though it had been pulled apart at the seams.

The tall figure turned, and a shaft of moonlight fell on the face of the intruder just as she was in the process of lifting one heavily booted foot to stomp down on the leg of the felled chair.

The woman's face, twisted and ugly with malice, was one that Riley knew.

Caution vanished in the path of the blind rage that overtook Riley at the sight of Geneva Myron. She'd nearly lost two of the most important people in her life tonight, and now Geneva was going to vandalize her grandmother's property on top of all that?

Not in *this* lifetime.

"You bitch!" Riley cried, throwing the door open with such force that it banged against the wall.

Geneva jumped and almost dropped her flashlight. The look of gape-mouthed astonishment on her face would have been comical if Riley hadn't been so angry.

"You've been doing this all along," Riley continued, stepping into the cabin. "You've been wrecking the cabins, and sneaking around the house at night . . . *why*? To scare an old woman? To make her think . . ." Her voice trailed off as realization dawned. "You were trying to scare my grandmother off of her own property, weren't you?"

Geneva, recovering from her initial shock, pulled herself up to her full height. She advanced toward Riley until they were almost face-to-face, two combatants in a showdown.

Riley, nearly standing on her tiptoes to bring herself up to the other woman's height, was too furious to back down. "Are you really so small-minded that you can't put up with a little extra activity for a few months out of the year?"

"A little extra activity? The kids scream all day and run all over the place, even right up into our yard. They . . ." Geneva stopped, and pulled herself together. "Besides, I don't even know what you're talking about. You're as crazy as she is. I was looking for Kirby. He got out a couple of hours ago and I haven't been able to find him."

As if on cue, Kirby barked in the distance. The sound came from the general direction of the Myrons' house.

"Sounds like Kirby found his way home," Riley said, her voice heavy with sarcasm. She glared at the other woman. "You've been destroying private property. This is vandalism, and—and terrorism. I don't know what all, but you'll be held accountable for your actions."

Still holding her flashlight, Geneva tried to push past, but Riley blocked her way. "Let me out," Geneva snarled.

Riley knew the sensible thing to do would be to let her go. She could call the police in the morning and report what she'd seen, and let the authorities take over from there. But she was too angry let it go so easily. "You're going to pay for the damage you've done, and I'll make sure everyone knows all about it—"

Her face twisted with fury, Geneva raised the heavy flashlight as though it were a club. She was a powerful woman, broadly built, and she towered over Riley by several inches. At last Riley understood that confronting this woman might not have been the wisest move on her part, but before she could react, or even raise an arm to defend herself, she was tackled from behind. Her body was hit with such force that the air was knocked from her lungs as she was propelled forward. Geneva stepped deftly out of the way, and Riley hit the small kitchen table hard enough to make stars dance before her eyes. Then the back of her parka was grabbed, and she was pulled up, held like a marionette whose strings had been cut.

She looked into the face of Duane Myron, and if Geneva had seemed dangerous, her son appeared homicidal. He shoved Riley hard against the wall. A picture fell to the floor, the glass in the frame shattering as he held her by the front of her parka, two handfuls of the down-filled garment bunched in his fists as he glared at her.

"Go home," he shouted, his spittle spraying Riley's face. "Things are fine here without you."

"Duane, stop," Geneva hissed. "This isn't the way." But she stood off to one side, flashlight still in her hand, and made no move to control him.

Never one to keep her big mouth shut, Riley struggled against Duane. "You're the ones who want the resort, aren't you? You're trying to get my grandmother to sell it to you. It won't work—even if a contract's been signed, I'll make sure you never get this place."

Duane looked back over his shoulder at his mother. She shrugged.

"Shut up, slut," he said to Riley, giving her a shake.

She tried to kick out at his shins with her boots, but couldn't get enough of a backswing to do any damage. Twisting and trying to free herself, she was no match for his wiry strength. "You had that purchase agreement made up and maybe my grandmother signed it, but it won't hold up in court," she gasped. "And I'll fight you every step of the way!"

Duane's lips curled into a malevolent smile. "You're as loony as your old granny."

"Don't play stupid. I found it, and I'm going to put a stop to it."

Duane looked at his mother again. "You have any idea what she's squealing about?"

Geneva shook her head. Then she moved past them, muttering, "Don't be long," to Duane as she left the cabin.

Now alone with Duane, Riley felt a surge of panic in her midsection, and she increased her struggles. At least with his mother here she'd believed that, though he might rough her up a bit, the abuse wouldn't get serious. That had all changed now.

His breath hot and foul, Duane pressed his body full length against her. Riley turned her face away from him. "You won't get away with this," she said. She managed to get one hand up and between them, and pushed against him as hard as she could. It made a small difference, but not enough.

"Away with what? You heard what my mother said—we were just out looking for our lost dog."

Then his expression changed to one of surprise, and he released Riley so quickly that the back of her head thumped against the wall. She almost slid to the floor, but caught herself in time, and she watched as Duane was lifted and flung aside as effortlessly as a bag of dirty laundry being tossed into a corner. He scrambled back crab-like until he could go no farther.

And Aaron stood there, tall and imposing, his expression grim as he fought the urge to kick the smaller man with the toe of his heavy boots. He turned to Riley. "Are you all right?" he asked.

She nodded, though she was shaking badly. "W-what are you doing here? Why aren't you in the hospital?"

"I didn't want to stay there. I wanted to be here with you so I checked out AMA—against medical advice." He glared down at Duane. "I'm glad I did."

Duane pushed himself to a standing position, but continued to cringe, as though expecting Aaron to come at him again. He looked at the open doorway, assessing his chances of getting through in one piece. Aaron took a step toward the man, but Riley put a hand on his arm.

"Let him go," she said. "We can deal with them tomorrow."

Aaron glowered. "But—"

"Please," she whispered. "I just want to go back inside the house and close the door. I can't take much more tonight."

Seeing his opportunity, Duane slinked past them, out of the cabin, and was swallowed up by the night before Aaron could grab him. Aaron watched, but didn't go after the man. He looked at Riley, and his expression softened. "It's been a hell of a day, hasn't it?" he said. He picked up the overturned chair.

Riley looked around, assessing the damage to the cabin.

"Most of it's cosmetic," she said after a minute, running a still-shaky hand through her hair. "What kind of people are they to do something like this? They've lived next door to my grandmother for two years. I'll bet they've seen the changes in her lately and knew what was happening. Maybe they've had a family member with Alzheimer's—which makes their actions all the more despicable."

Aaron helped her lock the front door of the cabin. "What were they trying to do?"

"Frighten her, make her life miserable," Riley sighed. "I don't know what motivates people like that. Gran tried to tell me someone was coming into the cabins and around the house, but I wouldn't listen. I still don't think they were bold enough to actually go into the main house, but they were able to get her confused and scared enough that she thought they had."

They went into the house together, where Riley shed her parka and boots.

The two sheets of paper were on the end table beside the sofa. She got the pages and, bracing herself, stood in front of Aaron. "I don't have the whole thing. When I was with Geneva and Duane in the cabin I was sure they were behind this, but they really didn't seem to know what I was talking about. *Someone* has made an offer on this property." She lifted her eyes to his. "Was it you?"

Aaron took the papers from her, his eyes quickly scanning the densely typed pages. Then he slowly shook his head. "No. I have no idea what this is about."

Riley dropped her face into her hands.

Aaron took her hands gently and pulled them away. "What did you think, Riley? That I would take advantage of your grandmother—a woman I like and respect?"

"I didn't know what to think. This whole day . . . I find out Gran is sick, and I don't know what I can do about it, or what the future will bring for either of us because of it. Then I find this . . ." She forced herself to look into his eyes. It was the hardest thing she'd ever done. "I had to ask. You understand that, don't you?"

He ran a hand over his face. "We've both made mistakes," he said. "What we need to do now is find the rest of that document. That will tell you who the offer came from, and when. Where did you find it first? That's where we should start looking."

"In a kitchen drawer, but I've looked through most of them

already."

"We'll search every inch of this house till we find the rest of it. I don't think she would have taken it out of the house. We'll start in the kitchen, and—"

"Not tonight," Riley interrupted. "We can look in the morning. For now I'm just so tired of it all, and I want to go to bed."

One dark eyebrow arching upward, Aaron said, "I have to admit I like that idea, but if we find this thing tonight you'll sleep easier. I don't want you having any more doubts about me."

Placing the palm of her hand against his chest, Riley knew that what she had to say was the truth. "I don't have any doubts, Aaron. You tell me you don't know where this came from, that's good enough for me."

"Are you sure about that?"

"Positivo," she said.

His lips curved up into a lopsided grin. "Then I propose we put this night behind us."

Riley nodded. "I agr—*umph!*"

He'd swooped down and kissed her so thoroughly that the sudden pressure of his mouth on hers halted whatever she'd wanted to say. She wrapped her arms around his neck, and he lifted her easily in his arms.

"Aaron!" she protested. "You just got out of the hospital—don't try to do too much too soon. You need to rest."

But he wasn't listening to her, any more than he'd listened to the nurses who'd tried to make him to stay in the hospital. "I'll rest when I'm dead," he said, heading for the stairs.

Her arms around his neck, she scolded, "Don't even joke about that."

He took her to her room and lay her down on the bed.

"I'm not joking. Right now I feel more alive than I have in years, and I don't intend to waste a minute of it." He lay beside her, propped up on one elbow. "I could stay here all night and just watch you sleep, you know that? Your face is endlessly fascinating to me."

Riley tugged at the top button of his shirt until it popped open. "Is that really what you want to do now that we have some time alone together? Watch me sleep? I would have expected you to have something more adventurous in mind."

Eyes blazing as he took her in, Aaron growled low in his throat. "I have a lot of things in mind, Red, but I don't want to be inconsiderate. You've had a tough night. You must be exhausted."

The second button popped free. "I was," she admitted. "But I seem to have gotten my second wind. Or maybe it's just that I'm so relieved that you're safe, all I want to do is put my hands on you and make sure you're really here with me." She'd worked most of the buttons free, and now Riley pushed the shirt open, admiring the broad chest she'd only recently become acquainted with. She stopped. "Where'd you get these clothes?" she asked, noticing for the first time that the plaid shirt was faded, and not the one he'd been wearing earlier.

Aaron looked down. "Oh, yeah. My stuff was still a mess. A buddy of mine works at the hospital. He found some old castoffs there for me."

She pushed the shirt from his shoulders, then leaned forward and pressed her lips to the center of his chest, right over his heart. Aaron inhaled sharply, then his fingers dug into her shoulders and he pulled her to him. With deft movements they shed their garments. Riley's pajamas went into a heap on the floor, on top of Aaron's borrowed clothing. They pushed the covers of the bed aside, so nothing kept them from exploring and enjoying the sight of each other's bodies.

She noted, with some dismay, that his strong arms were deeply bruised in spots. She kissed first one purpling area, then another, as though the touch of her lips could heal the damage, or at least take away the pain. Aaron put his hand in her hair, and each time her lips made contact with his skin he gave a profound groan of pleasure.

The horrors of the evening vanished in both their minds as they explored each other, learning anew what they'd begun a couple of nights earlier, deepening their commitment, taking in the increasingly familiar contours of limbs. Aaron ran a hand over Riley's skin, his touch light, as though he were seeing her with his fingertips. His hand traced the smooth line of the back of her thigh, down to the hollow behind her knee, then cupped her calf and pulled it over his hip. She moved to him, arching slightly so they melded together easily, the contact bringing a combined sigh that drifted in the air above them, filling the room with the music of their passion.

At one point a tear slipped free from Riley's eye, and Aaron, seeing it, caught it with the tip of his tongue.

"What's going on?" he asked, his voice a whisper in her ear. "I thought we were making each other happy."

"I never knew what I was missing out on," Riley sighed. She buried her face in his chest, as though to burrow into him. "But it could all slip away from me again. Nothing is permanent, I learned that tonight. Tomorrow it could all be gone again . . ."

"Stop," Aaron commanded, and his hand on the small of her back pressed her close. "We've had very little time alone together, but we're here now. Instead of worrying about what might or might not happen, let's just enjoy this night for what it is."

"What is this?" she asked, even though she knew she should stop questioning everything and just savor their time together.

But Aaron had an answer for her. "This," he said, "is a miracle."

SEVENTEEN

Stretching luxuriously in her bed, Riley watched as a shaft of early sunlight came through the window and cut across the comforter. She was alone in the bed, but it echoed with memories of the night before, and the hours she and Aaron had spent here.

She could hear him moving around downstairs, and she rolled over on her side to grab his pillow and pull it to her, burying her face in his masculine scent. If she could just stay right here forever, in this bed and knowing he'd be coming back to her soon, she'd be content for the rest of her life. That couldn't be, of course. Life goes on, the body has its needs and there are obligations to be met. But for a short time the fantasy lived in her heart, and she cherished it.

"Hey, sleepyhead." The mattress dipped as Aaron sat down next to her. He pulled the pillow from her face. "You planning to stay here all day?"

"If possible," she said, and burrowed under the covers so only her eyes peeked out at him. Her hair fanned out like an auburn veil.

"Not possible. I bring gifts." He held out a steaming mug of coffee.

"Oh, goody." Riley sat up and took it from him, sipping carefully at the hot liquid.

"That's not all." He held out his other hand, in which were several pieces of paper. "I found the rest of the document."

"Oh!" She set the coffee cup on the nightstand. "Where did you find it?" she asked, taking the papers from him.

"In your grandmother's sewing room, between some old patterns." His expression grew serious. "It's dated almost three weeks ago. And the name of the buyer is on there."

Riley eagerly scanned the top page, her eyes instinctively looking for a name among the figures, property description and legal mumbo-jumbo. Despite her belief of the night before— that Duane had not known what she was talking about when she'd accused him of trying to buy the resort—she nonetheless wouldn't have been surprised to see his or his mother's name there.

But their names were not listed. What she did see there made her gasp.

"Clay Johansen," she said.

"I've already called a friend of mine who's an attorney," Aaron said. "His office isn't open on Saturday, but when I explained to him what's going on he agreed to meet us there. Get up, beautiful, we have an appointment in less than an hour."

"I can find out if anything's been processed with one phone call to the courthouse, but I can't do that until Monday morning," Eli Edmondson told them. He was about Aaron's age, with a bristly mustache and casual attire that didn't seem to go with his profession, but he'd looked through the document they'd brought, clucking his disapproval the whole time. "I can tell you, however, that even with the info you've given me about your grandmother's health, Riley, this contract is considered valid. Unless she was declared incompetent at the time of the signing, or if she signed under duress, fraud or undue influence, this is a legally binding agreement."

Aaron reached out and took Riley's hand at this news. Eli's eyebrows went up, but he said nothing.

On their way to the lawyer's office Riley and Aaron had stopped at the hospital to see Bette. They'd found her awake and feisty, but also deeply disturbed by what had happened the evening before. After Aaron discreetly left the hospital room, Bette had confided to Riley that she was frightened by the realization that episodes such as the one she'd had the evening before were likely to become more frequent. Riley had done her best to reassure her grandmother that she'd do everything she could to help.

She had not brought up the subject of the documents.

She'd wanted to see first what the attorney would have to say about it.

"But the Alzheimer's," Riley said to Eli. "Doesn't that mean she's not competent to sign something like this?"

"No," Eli said. "Because you only got the diagnosis yesterday. Remember, I said *at the time of signing*." He leaned forward, his elbows on the desk. "It's not hopeless. You can fight the sale, and I think you'd have a pretty good chance of having a judge see your side of things at a hearing. I'll find out more on how to proceed on Monday. I doubt Clay Johansen has this kind of money at his disposal, so he's probably been to see his lender about borrowing the funds. One interesting thing I did notice . . ." He opened a big legal volume he'd brought down from his bookshelf. "That stretch of lakeshore was zoned residential twenty years ago. Your grandmother's resort property wasn't affected because it was there long before the zoning change, so it was grandfathered in. If someone else bought the property they could also maintain the property as a business under the same clause—*unless* they reverted it back to a private home only, without the rental cabins or the business aspect of it. If anyone did that, the property would then fall under the residential zoning laws, and it could never again be converted back to a business."

Riley sat up straighter in her seat. "That's what Clay wants," she said with certainty. "He wants to destroy the business and keep the land residential, which is less invasive to its natural state."

Eli shook his head. "This is a pretty expensive way to go about doing that."

"He's obsessed," Aaron said. "If he did get the property, and he closed the resort, no other businesses would be able to open up on that stretch of lake, right?"

"Not as long as it stays zoned residential," Eli agreed. "Do you really think he'd sink this kind of money into it just for that purpose?"

"Yes," Aaron and Riley both said at the same time.

Eli steepled his fingers in front of his face. "Like I said, I think you have a pretty good chance of getting this reversed in a hearing, especially if Bette says she didn't understand what she was signing. But it won't be a quick process. There's always a lot of paperwork involved in something like this. We'll have to get your grandmother's medical records from the clinic, and her doctor's diagnosis of probable Alzheimer's."

"I can get that for you," Riley said.

"It will all go a lot easier," Eli continued, "if Clay Johansen can be made to see the futility of fighting you on it. If he does relinquish any claim to the property, then the whole process will speed up considerably. In the meantime, someone should be assigned as your grandmother's legal guardian. I understand you live out of state, Riley. Are you going to be around to see this through?"

Riley looked at Aaron. In a few short days her life had changed in ways she never could have anticipated. She no longer thought of returning to Texas as "going home." She *was* home, she knew. Physically, with her grandmother in the big house by the lake, and in her heart, with Aaron.

Still holding her hand, Aaron waited for her response, his expression intense.

Riley gave his hand a little squeeze. "I'm not going anywhere," she told them both.

Outside on the sidewalk a few minutes later, Aaron pulled her to him. They were standing in front of his SUV, with winter-bundled Saturday shoppers walking past them, but as he looked at Riley's face it was as though the rest of the world faded away.

How had he ever thought he didn't have time for her in his life, that his business dealings were all-important? All of the property in Iowa meant nothing if he didn't have this woman with him.

"There's been so much going on that I haven't had the chance to tell you what I really want to tell you," he said, his arms around her. "I love you. I want you to stay here, and not just for your grandmother. I know that's important, and you're going to have a lot of responsibilities to shoulder... but I want you to stay here for *me*, as well."

Riley smiled up at him. "Say that again."

"Okay. You're going to have a lot of resp—"

She punched him playfully on the arm. "Not that. You know what I mean."

"I love you, Riley, and I want you to stay here with me."

"I like the sound of that." She leaned her head on his broad chest, closed her eyes and listened to the strong pounding of his heart. "I'll never get tired of hearing you say that."

He didn't say anything, but just waited, patiently.

"I love you too," she said at last.

"*That's* what I wanted to hear, Red."

"Don't call me Red."

"Admit it—you love it."

"Somehow, coming from you, I don't seem to mind," she admitted. "And, yes, I am also staying here for you. I'll have to tie up a few loose ends. I'll talk to my boss, see if I can lessen my workload and maybe do it long-distance, but if not . . ." She shrugged. "I'll figure something out. Somehow it doesn't seem very important any more."

Aaron picked her up and swung her around. He kissed her deeply on the lips, and Riley, her arms around his neck, kissed him right back. Several people stopped on the sidewalk to watch, with expressions of varying amusement. A little girl pointed and giggled, and her mother pulled her away, shushing her.

Looking around, Aaron whispered, "Shall we continue this discussion somewhere more private?"

"Is that what we're doing?" Riley asked. "Having a discussion?"

"For now," he said, and opened the door of the SUV for her.

EIGHTEEN

Four Months Later

The sand, clean and white, was warm between Riley's toes as she straightened the folding chair, one in a row of many. Her gauzy, knee-length dress billowed around her legs, and she looked around with satisfaction at the wedding preparations. The day couldn't have been better for an outdoor ceremony. The sun, bright in a cloudless sky, overlooked the wedding guests as they began to arrive. Jake Ross, accompanied by the terrier Kirby, who sported a wide pink ribbon around his neck, was leading the guests to their seats.

By the time Riley had settled her affairs in Texas and returned to her grandmother's house, the Myrons' place was up for sale and they'd moved out. Although he wouldn't admit it, Riley suspected Aaron had convinced them it would be wise to leave the area. They'd left Kirby behind, but Bette had taken him in, and soon after Chloe and Jake had fallen in love with the little dog, who was now a permanent member of the Ross household.

A few feet away Bette was fussing over a spray of fresh flowers and shells adorning the wooden trellis that had been placed close to the water's edge. She looked frustrated, and Riley went to her.

"These aren't tight," Bette said, adjusting a wire at the base of the flowers. As Bette continued to tug at the wire, the flowers began to work loose from the frame. "I don't want them to fall off right in the middle of the wedding."

Riley gently took her grandmother's hand from the flowers. "They won't, Gran," she assured her. "They'll be fine. You've done a wonderful job with these arrangements.

Remember how late we worked on them last night?"

Bette's expression clouded for a moment, then the sun shone through with a lovely smile. "We both did a good job. And you look so pretty."

"Thank you, Gran. You look pretty terrific yourself," Riley said. A light breeze swept through, and an auburn curl fell down on Riley's forehead. She pushed it back, tucking it in among the baby's breath and tea roses in her upswept hair.

Fitz appeared at their side. "Come over here and sit with me, Bette," he said, tucking her hand in the crook of his arm with tender care. "I've been saving a seat just for you."

"Is it time already?" Bette asked, and some of the worry returned to her expression.

"It's time, but all you need to do now is sit and enjoy the show. All the work is done."

At his soothing voice she relaxed again.

"Thanks, Fitz," Riley said.

She watched as he led Bette to an empty chair in the first row and sat with her. Re-tightening the wire on the flowers on the archway, Riley thanked heaven again for Fitz. In the past few months he'd been a rock, the stabilizing foundation Bette needed when her illness threatened to turn everything beneath her to quicksand. He hadn't abandoned Bette. Instead, he'd begun to come around even more often, to take her on outings or just to spend time with her. If at times he looked deeply saddened by the way her mind slipped away from them a little more each day, he always covered these brief moments with a steely resolve to enjoy their time together to the fullest.

Most days Bette did well. She was still busy with her genealogy group, and had made impressive advances in filling out the Harrison family tree. After being evaluated at the Mayo Clinic, she'd been put on a course of new medications that they still hoped would prove beneficial.

The two dozen folding chairs on the sand were filling up. It had been agreed early on to keep the ceremony simple, and having the wedding on the beach in front of the resort was ideal.

Aaron came up to Riley and took her hand. "It's time for you to stop worrying about every little detail, and have a seat," he said. He led her to the two remaining chairs beside Fitz and Bette, and they sat.

Chloe Ross, standing at a folding table off to the side, pushed a button on the CD player in front of her. Soft music began to play. Taking her duties very seriously, Chloe adjusted the volume until she was satisfied.

All heads, as though attached by a single string, turned to look up the pathway between the two sections of chairs.

A radiant Lauren, dressed in a flowing pink dress, held a spray of white roses as she stood with her hand on Stanley's arm. Lauren glowed like the flawless sky above, and Stanley beamed so broadly that it seemed his face would split in two as they walked down the aisle together. They reached the flowered archway, where a minister waited.

Riley blinked rapidly to fend back the tears that wanted to fill her eyes.

"Hey, no crying allowed," Aaron whispered.

Riley sniffled and pulled a tissue from the tiny purse at her waist. "I'm just so happy for them."

And for herself, as well. In the past few months so much had happened to change Riley's life. She'd left her job when it was determined she wouldn't be able to effectively do her work long-distance. She'd said good-bye to her friends, promised her mother and her sister that she'd be back to visit them—and had elicited promises from them that they'd come to Iowa— and she'd made the trip back, pulling behind her car a U-Haul trailer with all her possessions. She'd moved into her grandmother's house, and a month ago had launched her own website design company in town. Lauren had been her first client.

Eli had pointed out to Clay Johansen that, as a lifelong resident of the town, he would not benefit from the townspeople knowing—and Eli had assured Clay everyone *would* know—that he'd tried to take unfair advantage of Bette Harrison's condition. Clay had backed out of his efforts to buy Bette's property without the matter going before a judge.

It couldn't be helped that Riley and Clay ran into each other now and then, but they always nodded cordially and went their separate ways.

At the flowered trellis on the beach, the minister spoke familiar words to Lauren and Stanley, and Riley, being careful not to smear her mascara, dabbed at her eyes with her tissue. Since coming back to Iowa, she and Aaron continued to explore the depths of their feelings for each other. Feelings that seemed to grow stronger every day. They talked marriage at times, and both knew that's where they were headed, but for the time being they were content to enjoy the wonders of this love that had taken them both so much by surprise.

As though tuned in to her thoughts, Aaron leaned in close and whispered in her ear: "We're next."

On the beach, Stanley slipped a ring on Lauren's finger.

Riley turned in her seat and placed her palm on Aaron's chest. She felt the rock-solid beating there, and as always, was comforted by the steadiness of it. "My, what a big heart you have," she said.

Looking deeply into her eyes, Aaron said, "The better to love you with, my dear."

THE END

Other books by Jean Tennant:

Knee High by the Fourth of July: More Stories of Growing Up in and Around Small Towns in the Midwest (editor)
Shapato Publishing, October 2009

Walking Beans Wasn't Something You Did With Your Dog: Stories of Growing Up in and Around Small Towns in the Midwest (editor)
Shapato Publishing, August 2008

Olivia's Birthday Puppy
Sweet Memories Publishing, May 2008

Under the name Jean Simon:

Ghost Boy
Kensington, 1994

Orphans
Kensington, 1992

Sweet Revenge
Kensington, 1991

Wild Card
Kensington, 1991

Darksong
Kensington, 1990

Descendants
Warner, 1989

Playing House
Silhouette, 1986